VC

NW

H

LONG RIDER

Wes Stretton has ridden a long way to gain vengeance on Yoakum, whom he holds responsible for killing his friend. The trail takes him to the town of Buckstrap, where he meets the enigmatic Lana Flushing and walks straight into a range war between rival ranches, the Bar Seven and the Sawtooth. Someone knows of his arrival, however, and is out to bushwhack him. Then the foreman of the Sawtooth is shot. But was Stretton the intended target? And is Yoakum the culprit — or are things not quite what they seem?

COLIN BAINBRIDGE

LONG RIDER

Complete and Unabridged

LINFORD
Leicester

First published in Great Britain in 2017 by
Robert Hale
an imprint of The Crowood Press
Wiltshire

First Linford Edition
published 2020
by arrangement with
The Crowood Press
Wiltshire

A catalogue record for this book is available
from the British Library.

ISBN 978–1–4448–4538–9

Published by
Ulverscroft Limited
Anstey, Leicestershire

Set by Words & Graphics Ltd.
Anstey, Leicestershire
Printed and bound in Great Britain by
T. J. International Ltd., Padstow, Cornwall

This book is printed on acid-free paper

1

Wes Stretton drew his rangy sorrel to a halt within sight of the trading post. Below him the Locust River was a ribbon of green against the drab landscape with the rising hills as a backdrop. He put his hand to his chest and shoulder, grimacing as he did so. The gunshot wound was still troubling him. The fact that he had ridden a long way probably didn't help. He was pretty sure that he was still on Yoakum's trail, but maybe the proprietor of the trading post would be able to confirm it. If he was right, in all likelihood Yoakum would have stopped by. With a light touch of his spurs to the horse's flanks, he rode down to the store.

When he entered, he was greeted by a warm aromatic smell. Goods were piled high. A man stood behind a rough counter, talking with another man wearing grimy range gear. They both looked up at his arrival.

'Howdy,' he said

'Howdy.'

'Sure is hot,' Stretton said.

'We're lucky. There's usually a breeze comin' down off the hills.'

'Not today,' the man in range gear added.

Stretton glanced around. 'I could do with stockin' up on a few things,' he said.

'Take a look around,' the storekeeper replied. 'Just ask if you can't find anythin'. And while you're lookin' you could maybe use a mug of coffee? I've just made a pot.'

Stretton noticed two mugs standing on the counter. The man produced another from behind the counter and proceeded to pour.

'Sure is friendly of you,' Stretton replied.

He picked out a few items and handed them over before taking a drink. The coffee was good.

'Goin' far?' the man in range gear said.

'That depends,' he replied.

He took another sip of the coffee.

'What's the nearest town?' he asked.

'That'd be Buckstrap,' the man behind the counter replied.

Stretton thought for a moment.

'I guess this is the last place to pick up supplies before reachin' town,' he said.

'Or the first,' the man replied. 'Dependin' which way you're travellin'.'

'Do you get many customers?'

'I keep goin'. Why do you ask?'

'I'm lookin' for someone and I figured he probably came this way. If he did, it would be a whiles ago.'

'How long?'

'A couple of months maybe.'

'What's he look like?'

'Tall, thin, long straggly hair down to his shoulders.'

The two men looked at each other and the store owner scratched his chin.

'It ain't much to go on.'

'He has the lobe of an ear missin'. The right one. Oh, and he probably wore two guns.'

The storekeeper looked more closely at Stretton as if he suspected irony or was weighing which of his two comments was the more significant, while his companion's eyes dropped to Stretton's shooting irons.

'I can't say for sure,' the man resumed, 'but I seem to remember there was a feller maybe answerin' your description came in about then. There was another feller with him; small, kinda runtish.'

Stretton glanced at him with a puzzled expression on his face.

'Sounds like you didn't exactly warm to them.'

'I don't have any impression of the big man. There was something about the other one I didn't take to.'

'Was there some trouble?'

'No, nothin' like that. They bought a few things and then moved on.'

'Towards Buckstrap?'

The man shrugged. 'I guess so. There

ain't a lot of other places to go.'

Stretton swallowed the last dregs of the coffee.

'Thanks,' he said. 'For the information and the coffee.'

He picked up his purchases and made his exit. The eyes of the two men followed him and then the man in the range gear turned to his companion.

'I wonder why he's lookin'?' he said.

'I could hazard a guess,' the storekeeper replied. 'And I wouldn't want to be in the shoes of either of those *hombres* if he catches up with them.'

★   ★   ★

It was late afternoon when Wes Stretton hit town. He pulled up the sorrel outside the Cosmopolitan Hotel, dismounted and made his way inside. The desk clerk glanced at him.

'Been riding long?' he said.

There was a slightly supercilious look on his face, but his words made Stretton realize how unkempt and

5

trail-stained he must appear. He suddenly felt tired.

'Long enough,' he replied.

The man looked as if he was about to ask another question, but something about Stretton made him change his mind, and it wasn't the dust or the dirt. Instead he opened a ledger and slid it across the counter.

'How many nights?' he said.

Stretton thought for a moment.

'Just the one should do,' he replied.

When he had signed, he stepped outside and after putting up the sorrel at the livery stables, took a turn down the main drag till he found a barber shop and went inside. After having a shave and a hot bath he felt a lot better. He made his way to a clothing emporium and bought himself some new duds. Then he returned to the hotel where he changed and lay back on the bed.

After a while he sat up, built himself a smoke, and moved to the balcony which overlooked the street. Shadows

6

of evening were falling. From somewhere further along he heard the faint tinkling of a piano. He stubbed out what was left of his cigarette and went back inside the room. He had hung his gun belt over the bedstead and now he strapped it back round his waist. He drew the .44 Peacemaker from its holster and, almost absentmindedly, worked the spring on the hammer backwards and forwards a few times and then spun the cylinder before checking the loads. He replaced the gun, and with a last glance around the room, went out the door and down a flight of stairs. He glanced at the reception desk but the clerk wasn't there. The door to the dining room stood ajar and he had a glimpse of some people sitting at a table. He realized that he hadn't eaten in some time, but he didn't go in.

Once outside, he paused for just a moment before directing his steps in the direction of the saloon. He figured that if Yoakum was in town, it was there he would find him. He had come a long way from the Big Bend country. It was quite possible that he might be wrong, that Yoakum might have evaded him somewhere along the line. But he was encouraged by what the proprietor of the trading post had told him. Sooner or later they would meet, and now was just as likely a time as any other. At the thought, a faint quiver of anticipation caused him to lick his lips. His boots kicked up little clouds of dust which hung in the still air. He passed by a variety of false-fronted stores and offices, crossed a junction and approached the saloon. The single word 'Eagle' was scrawled in faded letters across the clapboard wall. The piano had stopped playing. He stepped up on to the boardwalk and pushed through the batwings.

The place was quiet, and his attention was immediately drawn to two men who stood at the bar. As he slowly advanced down the room, he saw the face of one of them reflected in the mirror behind the bar. It was Yoakum. There was no mistaking the long-drawn gaunt features,

8

the shoulder-length hair or the missing earlobe. His eyes met Stretton's, cold and without expression, and at Stretton's approach he turned slowly round. His coat was unbuttoned and drawn back to reveal twin gun-belts with tied-down holsters. He moved slightly away from the bar and at the same time his companion turned and shuffled almost imperceptibly to one side.

'Hello Yoakum,' Stretton said.

For a moment Yoakum said nothing. His blank eyes looked Stretton up and down before his mouth opened to reveal a broken line of chipped and blackened teeth.

'Do I know you?' he asked.

'Nope, but I know you.'

Yoakum turned to his companion.

'You hear that?' he said. The other man's lips curled in a wolfish grin. Stretton could hear the sound of chairs scraping against the floor behind him and the barman had moved surreptitiously to the end of his counter.

'You're the man who killed Ray

Crowther,' Stretton said. There was no reaction, but Stretton's acute senses told him that the conversation was about to end when suddenly a voice called out:

'That's enough boys. We don't want any trouble in here.'

It was a female voice, but it carried an air of authority and Stretton, taken by surprise, raised his eyes towards a flight of stairs at the side of the bar. A woman was standing half way down. She was big and buxom, but what impressed him even more than her figure was the sawed-down shotgun, which was pointed straight in his direction. The glance he gave her could have proved his undoing except for the fact that Yoakum was similarly distracted.

'Now why don't you boys finish your drinks and then leave?' she continued, looking directly at Yoakum and his companion. For a moment nobody moved or spoke, but Stretton noticed that she had shifted the shotgun almost imperceptibly and it was now aimed at Yoakum. His eyes flickered, moving between the woman and Stretton, and then he broke into an unconvincing laugh.

'Come on, Flynn,' he said. 'Seems like we're not wanted. There are plenty of other places to drink.'

He turned to the bar, picked up his glass of whiskey, and tossed what was left of it down his throat. Then, with an ugly stare, he pushed his way past Stretton and made for the batwings, followed by his companion. When the door swung to behind them, Stretton made to follow, but he was arrested in his movement by the woman's voice.

'Let them go,' she said.

She lowered the shotgun and began to descend the remaining stairs. When she came up to him, he realized he had missed his chance of following Yoakum.

'You're new in town,' she said. With her arrival, normal service seemed to have been resumed. She turned to the barman.

'Take this shotgun,' she said, 'and then bring a bottle of the best brandy over to my table.'

She handed the weapon across the counter before turning to Stretton.

'I wouldn't like you to get the wrong impression of our little town,' she said. 'At least let me offer you a drink.'

She exchanged glances with Stretton. For a moment he thought there was something familiar about her, but the notion quickly passed. He felt a little unsure of himself but when she began to move, he followed. She stopped at a little table in a secluded corner of the room, and almost without realizing what he was doing, he drew a chair back for her to sit on. When she had done so, he took the chair opposite. The barman came over with the bottle of brandy and two glasses, and at a glance from the woman he poured. When he had moved away the woman turned to Stretton.

'Well, let's drink to you being still alive,' she said.

Stretton grinned.

'I'll drink to that,' he replied.

He took a sip of the brandy. It was

rich and smooth and it hit the right spots.

'That's good,' he said.

'It ought to be,' she replied. 'I have it specially imported. From France. That's in Europe, a long ways from here.'

He looked at her.

'I figure I know where France is,' he said.

When he took another sip, he took the opportunity to look at her more closely. Although her make-up couldn't conceal the fact that she was well past the bloom of youth, she was still a handful of woman, and her purple velvet dress did little to hide the inviting contours of her figure.

'I take it you don't normally serve good brandy from France to the clientèle, so why are you giving it to me?'

She smiled but didn't immediately reply. He finished his glass and made to get up from the table but she put out an arm to detain him.

'There's no rush,' she said. 'See, there's plenty left in the bottle. Why not have some more?'

Before he could demur she had poured another glass.

'You haven't answered my question,' he said.

She topped up her own glass and then looked steadily at him.

'I am the proprietor of this establishment,' she said. 'I'd say that gives me the right to do what I like with my own property.'

'That still doesn't answer the question: why me?'

A faint smile passed across her face.

'Let's just say that I never took to Yoakum or his sidekick. On the other hand, I'd take an interest in anyone who seemed to feel the same way.'

Stretton couldn't help giving a slight start.

'You know Yoakum?' he asked.

'Sure. He's almost a regular. Once or twice he's come close to causing trouble, but nothing I couldn't handle.'

He looked at her more closely. For the first time he noticed some marks on her chin. They looked like tattooed lines. In the dusky half-light of the saloon he had failed to see them at first.

'What do you know about Yoakum?' he asked.

'That's easily answered,' she replied. 'He works for an outfit called the Bar Seven. The owner, Jed Claridge, is a friend of mine. And there's no secret about the fact that he can use a gun.'

Her eyes slid towards Stretton's revolvers.

'Maybe that ain't always such a bad thing.'

'Why do you say that?'

'The Bar Seven isn't the biggest ranch around here. That's the Sawtooth. It's run by a man called Lindop, Rex Lindop. Both of them have as much graze and more cows than they know what to do with, but that don't make any difference to either of 'em wanting more. I don't take sides. If they want to bring in gunslingers, that's their business. Just so long as they don't go thinkin' they can use their guns in my saloon.'

She paused and looked again at Stretton.

'I don't know why I'm telling you this,' she said.

'Because I asked,' he replied.

She took a sip of her drink.

'I've being doing too much talking,' she said. 'Now what about you? What are you doing in these parts? What's your interest in Yoakum?'

He thought for a moment, unsure whether to prevaricate, but he had a feeling she would soon detect any signs of insincerity. Besides, what would be the point?

'Back in Texas,' he said, 'I worked for an outfit called the Hog Eye. There was a dispute with another ranch about water rights. To cut a long story short, it led to shooting and a friend of mine got killed. Yoakum was the man responsible.'

She shrugged. 'That's unfortunate, but it doesn't really explain why you've come all this way looking for him. These things happen.'

16

'He was bushwhacked,' he said. 'Shot in the back. I was the one that found him.'

'How do you know Yoakum was responsible?'

'I know. There was evidence. There was even an eye-witness. I took a bullet myself in that affair. That might have come from Yoakum too, but I can't be sure.'

'This man Yoakum sounds rather careless,' she remarked.

'How do you mean?'

'Well, you've just told me about the eye-witness, and you seem to have tracked him as far as Buckstrap without too much difficulty.'

'I would have caught up with him before now, but I was laid up for a spell. It took a while to recover from the gunshot. I got the scars to prove it.'

'I'll take your word for it,' she said. 'At least, for now.'

There was a pause in the conversation. The saloon was filling up.

'So,' she continued eventually, 'what

do you intend doin'?'

He slung back the last of the brandy.

'You say Yoakum works for a ranch called the Bar Seven,' he said. 'Where do I find it?'

'You're thinking of going after Yoakum? Is that wise? He knows now that you're here. He'll be expecting you. If what you've told me is right, you'd be riding straight into trouble.'

'I came here to do a job. I aim to get on with it.'

She didn't reply immediately. When she did, she seemed to have taken a different tack.

'You might have noticed these marks on my chin,' she said. She leaned forwards so her face was less in shadow.

'I haven't told you my name yet,' she continued. 'It's Flushing, Lana Flushing. Leastways that's one name. I've got another one. It's Hualga.'

He nodded.

'If I'm correct, that means Moon. It's a nice name.'

She threw him a quizzical glance.

'You surprise me. Yes, it means Moon. I spent some time with the Mojave.'

'I could have guessed that much,' he replied.

'What? You mean these markings?'

'Ornamentation,' he replied. 'It all depends on your point of view.'

She smiled.

'It's all a long time ago now. I was captured by Tonto Apaches and sold to the Mojave when I was a girl. I spent some years with the Mojave. I became the wife of one of their chiefs. I might have been there yet, but things turned out differently. I don't regret any of it. It might seem strange to you to hear me say it, but they were good years.'

'I don't have to imagine it,' he said. 'I've spent time with the Indians too. But why are you telling me this? It's none of my business.'

'I'm telling you this because it has a bearing on what you've just told me.'

'I don't understand.'

'Well, I'm not altogether sure myself, but I guess it's like this. Things happen in life. They seem bad but they turn out good. They turn out to have been for the best.'

'I still don't follow.'

'Right now you want to get even with Yoakum. But can you be altogether sure that you're right about him? Yoakum is a hired gun, workin' for the Bar Seven. I know Jed Claridge, the owner of the Bar Seven. He's a friend of mine. He's a good man.'

'Then why has he got men like Yoakum in his employ?'

'That's just my point. Maybe you've got things wrong. Or rather, maybe you ain't seeing everything quite straight. Maybe you don't know the full story. Maybe you should take more time before you rush to vengeance. If you're right after all, you won't have lost anything.'

Stretton was silent. He still wasn't sure whether he had understood the woman aright. After a few moments he asked her another question.

'Are you sayin' I should stick around for a while?'

She looked closely at him.

'It wouldn't hurt,' she said. 'Who knows, you might find things turn out better than you might have expected.'

He sat puzzling her words. He felt a certain reluctance to leave her, but she solved that matter by getting to her feet herself.

'I have to go now,' she said. 'The place is getting busy. Think about what I've said.'

She began to move away, and then stopped.

'You know my name, but you haven't told me yours.'

He nodded and gave her the information.

'Well, Mr Stretton,' she said, 'perhaps I'll be seeing you again.'

She walked to the bar, her long dress rustling. His eyes followed her. She began to mount the staircase, and when she was gone at a turn of the stairs, he got to his feet and made his way to the batwings. He pushed through them and stood for a long moment on the boardwalk, breathing in the cool night air. He felt oddly shaken. His conversation with Lana Flushing had unsettled him, and he didn't know why. Sure, she was quite a specimen of her sex, but that wasn't it. As he mulled over her words, he still wasn't sure that he understood her drift. There was an enigmatic quality about both her and her conversation.

A few more moments passed, and then he stepped down from the boardwalk past the horses tethered outside the saloon. He turned aside and began to walk back towards the hotel. A few store lights burned, but the darkness was gathering and the street was quiet. He had almost reached the junction where a side street intersected the main drag when he heard a shout from behind him and stopped to turn round. At the same moment there was a stab of flame and a shot rang out, rapidly followed by a second, and a couple of bullets went singing by his head. Instantly he dropped to the ground and rolled into the shelter of the boardwalk. A third shot boomed and the bullet ripped into the dirt nearby, sending up a plume of dust. He drew his own weapon and fired back, straining his eyes to try and catch some sign of movement, but there was nothing to be seen. Looking in the direction of the Eagle, he saw two figures gesticulating. His immediate thought was that they were trying to catch his attention, but it soon became apparent that they were arguing with each other. Their voices were raised, but as quickly as the fracas had begun it came to an end, and the two men staggered arm in arm back into the saloon.

He turned his attention back to the intersection. Seconds passed, dragging their heels, turning slowly into minutes. He still couldn't see anything and although he strained his ears to catch any sounds, couldn't hear anything suspicious either. Then, after what seemed an aeon of time, he heard the clatter of hoof-beats coming from a little distance. They quickly faded into the night. When he was satisfied that his attacker had gone, he got back to his feet and ran to the approximate spot where he had seen the stab of flame. The dust was scuffed, and he quickly found the imprints of a pair of boots. He followed them along the street till he came to a hitching rail outside a bank. It was fairly apparent that whoever had taken the shots had returned the short distance to his horse which had been tied there, and made his getaway.

Satisfied that there was nothing further to be learned, Stretton retraced his steps and carried on walking till he reached the hotel, where he made his way to his room. He rolled a smoke and lay down on the bed to try and gather his scattered senses. Questions were forming in his mind, jostling one another, but foremost among them was the obvious one: who had fired those shots? It was pure luck that he had stopped in his tracks, distracted by the noises made by the quarrelling pair outside the saloon. If he hadn't done so, he would almost certainly be dead.

The initial conclusion was that it must be Yoakum. He wished he had checked the horses at the hitch rack. It would have been interesting to see if any of them carried a brand and if so, whether it was missing subsequently. As far as he could tell, only one person had been involved in the shooting incident. If that person was Yoakum, then what had become of his sidekick? If it wasn't Yoakum, who else could have a grudge against him? Who would have known he was even in Buckstrap? Whichever way he looked at it, it made no sense. And on top of all that, there was still Lana Flushing.

He was still troubled by her. He couldn't work her out. One thing was for sure, though. Even if she hadn't suggested that he stick around for a while, the way things had worked out, he would be doing so anyway. He hadn't come this far only to walk away when he had found his man. He needed to confront Yoakum. If Yoakum had taken those pot shots at him, there was even more reason to do so now. That meant paying a visit to the Bar Seven. He let out a sigh. When he had ridden into town things had seemed fairly straightforward. Now he wasn't so sure any more. The ground seemed to be moving under him, and he couldn't quite place his finger on the reason why.

Preoccupied with these thoughts, he suddenly realized that he was hungry. Some time had elapsed since he had left the hotel earlier to make his way to the Eagle Saloon, but maybe the dining room would still be open. He got to his feet and made his way to the door and then stopped. His keen ears had picked up the sound of footsteps at the top of the stairs. Taking his revolver, he waited behind the door. The footsteps passed along the corridor and came to a halt outside his room. After a moment there came a rap on the door. Without ado, Stretton seized the handle and flung the door open. Standing outside was a tall, thin man with a drooping moustache and greying hair. On his chest he wore a star. He appeared to be entirely unruffled.

'Mr Stretton?' he said.

Stretton nodded.

'You won't need the shooter,' the marshal continued. 'Mind if I come in?'

Without waiting for a reply he pushed past Stretton, who turned and followed him into the room, closing the door behind him. His gun belt was hanging from the bed-post and he placed the gun back in its holster.

'My name is Malone,' the man said. 'I'm marshal of Buckstrap.'

'You already seem to know my name,' Stretton replied.

'I got it from the hotel register,' the marshal said.

'Won't you take a seat?' Stretton suggested.

Malone shook his head. 'Like I said, I won't take up much of your time. In fact, I'll be very brief. I want you out of town by noon tomorrow.'

Stretton grinned.

'I think you must be mixin' me up with somebody else. I only just arrived in town. My plans involve stayin' around for a few days.'

'Then you'd better change your plans. This ain't a request. It's an order. If you're still here after the deadline, I'll be obliged to arrest you and put you in jail.'

'On what charge?' Stretton said.

'Try carrying sidearms, public affray, disturbin' the peace. They'll do for a start.'

'I haven't done anythin' against the law.'

'I'd say that firin' a weapon in a public place is a pretty serous offence.'

Stretton looked at the marshal.

'I don't know quite what you're drivin' at,' he said. 'It's true I was the victim of an attack earlier this evening.'

'So if I took a look at your gun, I'd find it hasn't been used recently?'

Stretton hesitated. 'I fired one shot in reply,' he said. 'I had no choice. Someone tried to dry-gulch me.'

The marshal grunted. 'Just make sure you've left town by noon tomorrow,' he said.

'And what if I don't?'

'I think I've already answered that.'

Stretton felt resentment begin to stir in him.

'What's this all about?' he said.

Malone grinned. His teeth were remarkably white and sharp.

'Just move on,' he replied. 'That way, everybody's happy.'

'Maybe not everybody.'

'What do you mean?'

Stretton had been thinking of Lana Flushing, but he only replied:

'Everybody except me.'

'You've been warned,' the marshal replied. 'Don't let there be a next time.'

He turned and walked away. Stretton listened to his footsteps till they faded away on the stairs. Then he sat down on the edge of the bed and rubbed his hands through his hair. As if he didn't have enough to think about already. Now he had a whole lot more, and none of it seemed to make much sense. What was behind the marshal's warning? Was it something to do with the Bar Seven? Or even the Sawtooth? He was a stranger in Buckstrap, yet somehow he seemed to be known. Maybe the marshal just didn't take to strangers. He spent some time racking his brains but could come up with no answer. Despite his hunger, he suddenly felt very tired. Without getting undressed he lay flat on the bed and drifted gradually into a fitful sleep.

2

When he awoke, he felt surprisingly refreshed. Sunlight slanted through the doorway giving on to the balcony. He got to his feet and quickly performed his ablutions before making his way to the dining room, where he was relieved to find a number of people in the process of eating breakfast. He took a vacant table and placed his order. By the time he had consumed a big plate of ham and eggs with grits and downed a couple of mugs of strong black coffee, he was feeling even better.

During the course of the night, his brain had come up with some answers to his immediate problems. Instead of heading for the Bar Seven, as he had originally intended, he would make for the Sawtooth. That way he might hope to learn more about the situation between Lindop and Claridge without the risk of running into Yoakum. That would come later. Before doing so, however, he would settle up at the hotel and avoid any trouble with the marshal. He didn't relish the prospect of possibly ending up in the jailhouse. He could always make camp somewhere out of town. It was more or less a way of life with him. In fact, he didn't feel altogether comfortable having a roof over his head for any length of time. As he drank his third mug of coffee, he found himself thinking of Lana Flushing. At some point, he would have to make contact with that lady again.

When he had finished eating, he got to his feet and made his way to the foyer to pay his bill. Since he had only registered for one night anyway, it was quickly settled. Then he made his way towards the livery stable where he had left his horse. It was a fine day and he was still feeling good. When he got there, the ostler wasn't around. Instead, he found an old-timer outside in the corral forking hay.

'Howdy,' Stretton said.

The man's mouth was twisted as it worked a chew of tobacco. He was old and wrinkled but his eyes were bright. He spat out some juice before replying.

'Howdy. Figured you'd be back. That sorrel of yours is a nice horse.'

'Which way is it to the Sawtooth?' Stretton asked.

The oldster laid his fork against a rail of the corral and came closer.

'Why do you ask?' he said.

'I'm lookin' for a job,' Stretton replied. Until that moment the thought had not occurred to him. Suddenly it seemed like a good reason. The oldster's eyes dropped to Stretton's 44s.

'What kind of a job you got in mind?' he said.

Stretton shrugged. 'I can put my hand to most things around a ranch,' he said.

The oldster spat once more and then looked at Stretton with eyes that were suddenly cold.

'You ain't foolin' me,' he said. 'If your

33

gun's for hire, that's just fine. You'll make good money, whether you're ridin' for the Sawtooth or any other spread.'

'Such as the Bar Seven,' Stretton interposed.

'Sure. The Bar Seven. You'll be in good company either way.'

Stretton raised his eyes to glance at the stable and the corral.

'What's goin' on round here?' he asked, turning back to the oldster.

The man emitted something that sounded like a growl but was probably a sardonic laugh.

'I figure you don't really need me to tell you. And what's more, I don't give a damn about who's wrong and who's right. I'm too old for all that. It'll be the same story in the end. People will die, but nothin' will change.'

'Why should people die?'

'Because of people like you.' The oldster paused. 'No, that ain't fair. Because things are the way they are, I guess. Nobody ever thinks they have enough. Nobody ever learns.'

'Who are you talkin' about?'

'Lindop. Claridge. The names are interchangeable.'

'How do you mean?'

'Whoever is top dog now, sooner or later it'll be someone else. There's always someone wants to have more — more land, more cattle — even if they don't know what to do with it.'

Stretton considered his words for a moment.

'You think I'm hiring myself out as gunman,' he said. 'Well, that ain't true. You got it wrong.'

The oldster chuckled. 'We'll see,' he said. 'Like I say, I'm old. None of it concerns me any more.'

Stretton looked at him again.

'You really mean that?' he asked.

By way of reply, the oldster picked up his implement once more and began to fork hay again.

'Your horse is ready,' he said, without looking up.

★　★　★

It was mid-afternoon when Stretton caught his first sight of the Sawtooth. The oldster's directions were clear, and he found his way without any problems. Even before he reached the ranch he could tell that it was prosperous from the condition of the cattle he saw. They were sleek and well fed. Out of habit, he checked some of the markings. They all carried the Sawtooth brand. Only once did he see a rider, but he was quickly gone behind a clump of trees.

The ranch-house itself was a substantial two-storey stone-built structure with a broad veranda. Behind it were a considerable number of outbuildings. For a time Stretton sat his horse to observe before touching his spurs to the sorrel's flanks. As he came through the yard, a man emerged and placed himself in his path. Stretton dismounted and tied his horse to a hitch-rail.

'Howdy,' he said.

The man didn't reply so Stretton carried on talking.

'I'm looking for the ramrod,' he said.

The man looked him up and down.

'I'm the ramrod,' he replied.

Stretton held out his hand but the man ignored him.

'I'm lookin' for work,' Stretton said. 'I'm willin' to do anythin'.'

The man continued to look at him. His eyes were cold.

'You're takin' a big chance ridin' out here,' he said.

'Like I said, I'm looking for a job.'

'There are no jobs.'

'That's not what I heard.'

'I don't care what you heard. You'd better get back on your horse and get the hell out of here while you can.'

Stretton waited for a moment. He wasn't sure how to proceed and was just about to move when the ranch-house door opened and a man appeared smoking a cigar. He stepped on to the veranda and advanced so he was just above Stretton and the ramrod.

'What is this, Rimmer?' he said.

'It ain't nothin', Mr Lindop,' Rimmer

replied. 'I was just showin' this saddle bum off the premises.'

Lindop turned his attention to Stretton.

'You'd do well to do what he tells you,' he said.

'That's fine and dandy,' Stretton replied. 'I just thought . . . '

He paused. 'Well, what did you think?' Lindop prompted. Stretton decided to push his advantage.

'Somebody tried to shoot me yesterday,' he said. 'I got a hunch that whoever it was is connected to the Bar Seven. I kinda figured . . . '

'You want me to deal with him?' Rimmer interrupted.

Lindop looked at him and shook his head. 'No,' he replied. 'It's OK. You've done fine, but leave this to me.'

Rimmer looked from Lindop to Stretton and back again. He didn't look happy.

'You sure, Mr Lindop?'

'Yeah. Take his horse over to the corral and then get on back to the bunk-house.

I'll send for you if I need you.'

Rimmer turned on his heels and began to walk away. When he had disappeared from view round the corner of the ranch-house, Lindop turned to Stretton.

'You'd better come on in,' he said.

Stretton stepped up to the veranda and followed Lindop inside. The room he entered was spacious and well appointed, the furniture sparse but tasteful. What attracted his attention was a heavy chandelier which dominated the centre of the room, and a large cabinet containing an impressive array of bottles and glasses.

'Whiskey?' Lindop asked.

Without waiting for a reply he strode over to the cabinet and poured a couple of drinks.

'Take a seat,' he said.

Stretton did as he suggested and took a long sip of the whiskey. It tasted very good. Even to his unpractised palette it was obviously an expensive brand. As he did so, he looked at Lindop more closely. The man was quite short but he gave an impression of strength. His hair was white and closely cropped, and he sported a goatee beard. Stretton wasn't sure how to take things. His reception at the Sawtooth was certainly mixed, and it wasn't what he had expected. It was Lindop who broke the silence.

'So,' he said, 'you were saying something about being shot at. Might I ask where and when this incident took place?'

'Last night,' Stretton replied. 'In town.'

Lindop took a sip of his drink.

'And you seem to think the Bar Seven might be involved. What gives you that impression? If you're new to the area, how do you even know about the Bar Seven?'

Stretton thought quickly before replying. He wasn't sure of his position, but it seemed sensible to let Lindop know as little as possible of events prior to the incident itself. In a few brief words he outlined what had occurred.

'You think this man Yoakum might be

responsible?' Lindop asked.

'Seems like too much of a coincidence otherwise.'

Lindop sipped some more of the whiskey.

'Is that why you've come here?' he said.

'I heard some talk. I gather there's trouble brewing. That bein' the case, it seemed to me like you could always use some extra help.'

'I've got plenty of range hands.'

'That ain't entirely what I meant.'

This time it was Lindop's turn to regard Stretton's 44s.

'It's no secret that there's a range war brewing,' he said.

'And it looks like Yoakum is on the other side,' Stretton interposed.

Lindop seemed to consider this remark before replying.

'OK. I'm not sure about you, Stretton, but the way things are, I'd rather have you here than somewhere else. Who knows, you might offer your services to another ranch, maybe even the Bar Seven.'

'I ain't likely to do that.'

'Maybe not, but things don't always work out like we expect. Get on over to the bunk-house and have a word with Rimmer. He'll tell you what to do.'

'He didn't seem to take to me exactly.'

'Rimmer's fine. He won't give you any trouble, not now I've decided to take a chance with you. Leaving aside anything else we've been saying, you'll be working real hard. I take it you've got experience?'

'Sure. Plenty of it. I'm an old hand.'

'Then I'll expect you to prove it.'

Stretton finished the whiskey and put his glass down before getting to his feet. 'Thanks,' he said.

With a nod he made for the door and went outside. For a moment or two he stood on the balcony, enjoying the breeze. Then he went down the steps and headed for the bunk-house.

When he opened the door, the first person he saw was Rimmer. He was talking to another man and they both looked up at his approach. It seemed as if Rimmer had been expecting him. On the other hand, he may have just been following Lindop's instruction to wait around till he was sent for.

'I don't want any trouble,' Stretton said.

'What makes you say that?'

'It's pretty obvious you don't like me.'

Rimmer shrugged. 'I just do as Mr Lindop says,' he replied.

'In that case, you can show me my bunk.'

Rimmer indicated a vacant bunk with a nod of his head.

'I'll go get my bedroll,' Stretton said.

He stepped to the door, but before he could open it Rimmer's voice rasped:

'You know how to handle that 44?'

'If I have to.'

Rimmer chuckled.

'Oh, you'll have to,' he said 'You can take that from me.' He paused for just a brief moment. 'And get one thing straight. I'm the boss around here.

What I say, goes. You got that? You do whatever I tell you to do.'

'I didn't imagine things would be any different.'

'Good. That's understood. Then before you go I'll give you your instructions for tomorrow.'

Stretton stepped back inside for a moment. Rimmer moved a few paces, bent down, and stood up with a burlap bag in his hand.

'Here, take this,' he said.

He handed Stretton the bag. Stretton peered inside. It contained a pair of fence pliers, a narrow hatchet, and what appeared to be an old boot top sewed at the bottom and filled with staples and a small coil of stay wire.

'Fence ridin',' Rimmer snapped. He gave directions. Stretton realized he was being victimized. He was being given a menial chore that any open-range cowboy would have balked at.

'The job might take a while to complete. You'll find a line cabin out there with some basic supplies. Start off real early and make sure you do a good job.'

Stretton took the bag and flung it on his bunk. Then without further ado, he went out the door and made his way to the corral. His sorrel was there together with a few other ponies. It came over to him and he stroked its nose in a desultory fashion. His thoughts were elsewhere. He was beginning to wonder just what he had got himself into. When he had started out that morning, he had no intention of winding up being in Lindop's employ. He had almost sleep-walked into taking on a job with the Sawtooth, and he had no idea where it would lead him.

One thing seemed certain: a range war was building up. He had a sudden feeling of déjà vu. The same thing had happened where he was before, and as a consequence, he was here now seeking Yoakum. He was acting almost by instinct. However, getting even with Yoakum remained his priority. At least he had a berth for the time being. He would see how things worked out. He was also out of the way of the marshal. He wondered what that lawman's reaction would be if he knew he was riding for Lindop.

* * *

He awoke early the following morning. People were still sleeping in the other bunks, and outside it was dark. He made his ablutions and then went to the corral where he found the sorrel. The first tinges of light were just touching the horizon as he rode out of the yard. No one was about. As he got further from the ranch-house, he began to see indistinct outlines of cattle, some singly, others in groups. It wouldn't be long till the round-up.

Although his plans were very uncertain, he was already beginning to think in terms of the routines of the ranch. Rimmer had been deliberately vague about what his task entailed, but he figured that once he arrived at the relevant section of the range, he would be able to work it out for himself. Various things could happen to make fence riding necessary. Judging from the equipment with which he had been supplied, it would probably be a question of hammering staples into posts where the wires had begun to sag. It was work of a type with which he was not too familiar; like a lot of other people, he regretted the change from open range to fences. Before doing any fence riding, he intended finding that line cabin and fixing himself some breakfast.

As he rode, he instinctively kept his eyes skinned for anything going on around him. It was second nature. A man's safety depended on being alert. His ears were also strained to pick up sounds. It wasn't just a question of possible danger. The bawl of a cow in a coulee might indicate that it was in trouble. The shadows were being dispelled by the gathering rays of the risen sun, and the only sounds were the thud of his horse's hoofs and the creak of leather. He continued to see occasional cattle, but they were becoming fewer and fewer, and after a time he realized he was no longer coming across them. It raised a question: if there were no cattle out this way, then why had Lindop bothered to build fences?

There could be other reasons. Maybe it was just a matter of delineating the boundaries of his property. In all likelihood the gathering feud between the Sawtooth and the Bar Seven was a question of land rights. The land across which he was riding was free range land, and Lindop was deliberately taking it over and fencing it off. What was on the opposite side? Was it open range or did the land belong to a neighbouring ranch? Could it be the Bar Seven? It was quite likely. Even if other ranches were involved, the main antagonists in the impending range war appeared to be the Sawtooth and the Bar Seven.

He continued riding for a considerable time before he reached the fence. The fact that he had covered some distance since leaving the ranch-house seemed, if anything, to confirm his feeling that it was open range, or probably had been until recently. As he had suspected, the fence was new. The cedar posts were fresh and the barbed wire glinted in the sunlight. It had obviously only recently been strung. Alternative posts had been placed on opposite sides of the wire to give additional strength, and corner posts were braced with barbed wire twisted into cables with their ends buried deep in the ground. One thing was for sure. There was no good reason to have sent him out with the fence-mending equipment. So what was Rimmer up to? The answer became clear as he continued riding along the line of the fence and arrived at a spot where it had been broken and damaged. He had been thinking that he had been sent on a wild goose chase, but that wasn't the case.

He was feeling hungry. It had been very early when he set out, and now the sun was high. The sorrel needed rest. Rimmer had mentioned a line cabin, but there was no sign of it. If the old boundary line had been altered, it was probably somewhere behind him, if it existed at all. Abandoning the idea of finding any kind of a cabin, he looked about for a suitable place to stop. Suddenly he tensed. Off in the distance he could see some buzzards circling in the sky. He brought the sorrel to a halt and reached for his field glasses. He put them to his eyes and scanned the terrain in the direction of the birds. There was something lying on the ground. Quickly, he replaced the glasses and without further ado, set off towards the object he had just seen.

He knew what to expect. As he drew near, he could see it was the body of a man. Most of the buzzards were still circling, but a couple of them which had landed nearby flapped up at his approach. He brought his horse to a halt and leaped from the saddle. The man was lying face down, but here was no obvious injury. It was only when he gently turned him over that he saw a bullet wound in the upper right chest area. But what really took him aback was the face of the victim: it was Rimmer. At the same time he realized that Rimmer was still breathing.

Instantly he returned to the sorrel and got out his medicine bag, the flask of whiskey, and a knife. Taking no time to consider the situation, he poured whiskey over the wound and then began to probe with the knife. It didn't take long for him to find the bullet and dig it out. He couldn't tell if Rimmer was feeling any pain. His face was twisted and at one point he murmured something. When Stretton had finished, he poured more whiskey on the wound and then bound it up, using his bandana. As far as he could tell, Rimmer had been lucky. The bullet had lodged itself in a fleshy area and no bones appeared to be broken. He took a swig of whiskey himself and then rolled himself a cigarette to sit it out till Rimmer returned to consciousness.

He decided there was no point in

trying to move Rimmer, but he got his blanket to make a makeshift pillow for his head. After a time he got to his feet to take a look around. He found tracks of two horses. He guessed they were those of Rimmer and his assailant. One set of tracks came from the direction he had come earlier. The other set, which he assumed were those of Rimmer's attacker, led towards the broken fence. There was just enough in the way of scrub and bushes to provide cover for a bushwhacking, but he could make no sense of it.

He gave up trying to figure it out, and instead set about gathering the materials for a fire. When it was sufficiently well established, he laid a few slabs of bacon in the pan, filled his old iron pot with water and positioned it over the flames. He had just laid his food on a platter and was pouring coffee into his tin cup, when he heard a grunt and looked round to see in the firelight that Rimmer was beginning to stir. He made an effort to sit up, groaned, and then sank back again.

'Take it easy,' Stretton said.

Rimmer turned his eyes on him, as if he had only just become aware of his presence.

'Stretton,' he muttered.

'Yeah.'

Rimmer struggled to sit up again and this time succeeded.

'My shoulder hurts like hell,' he said.

'That isn't surprisin'. I just dug a bullet out of it.'

Rimmer glanced down at Stretton's makeshift dressing.

'What happened?' he said.

'You've been shot. Someone obviously doesn't like you. Must say I've got some sympathy with him.'

A faint flicker of a smile passed briefly across Rimmer's twisted features.

'Hell, it hurts,' he repeated. He paused for a moment and then nodded in the direction of the fire. 'I could use some of that.'

'Grub?'

'Nope, just coffee.'

Stretton rose and walked over to the sorrel. He returned carrying a flask and another cup. He poured coffee into the cup and then laced it with whiskey from the flask.

'Can you manage?' he asked as Rimmer reached for the cup. The ramrod nodded, took the cup in his left hand and swallowed a few mouthfuls.

'I did my best to clean up the wound,' Stretton said. Rimmer took another swig, grimacing with the effort.

'It might be an idea to get you to a doc,' Stretton added.

Rimmer shook his head. 'I'll be OK,' he said. 'I just need a bit of time.'

Stretton cleared his plate and poured another cup of coffee for himself. Then he got out his bag of Bull Durham and built cigarettes for himself and Rimmer. When he had inhaled deeply, he turned to the injured man.

'None of this makes any sense to me,' he said.

'Me neither,' Rimmer replied.

'Maybe not, but you can at least

explain what in tarnation you're doin' here.'

Rimmer returned Stretton's enquiring look.

'I could ask you the same question,' he said.

'Don't try that one,' Stretton replied. 'You know perfectly well what I'm doin' here since it was you who gave the orders for me to ride out this way.'

'I guess I did at that,' Rimmer replied.

'Those fences . . . ' Stretton began but Rimmer cut him short.

'You probably think they're ours. They ain't. They're Bar Seven fences. That's Bar Seven range on the other side. Leastways, it is now. Used to be free range.'

'I reckoned it was the other way,' Stretton said. He thought for a moment.

'If they ain't ours, why try to fix 'em?'

'Some cattle did that damage. Ours or theirs, it doesn't matter. The way I figured it, if a range war is comin', it might be to our advantage to keep the fence repaired.'

'Looks like I figured it all wrong.'

'That's the way a lot of folks think,' Rimmer replied. 'Just because the Sawtooth is the biggest ranch doesn't mean it always has to be in the wrong. And now that the Bar Seven has fenced off all that land, the Sawtooth probably ain't even the biggest any more.'

Stretton scratched at his chin.

'You still haven't said what you're doin' here,' he said.

'I rode out this way last night. I had reason to believe that before they finished that fence, the Bar Seven ran off some Sawtooth cattle. So I went and took a look. Sure enough, I was right. I didn't have to go far to see cows carryin' the Sawtooth brand. I guess somebody must have seen me.'

'You figure that was the person who shot you?'

'Can you think of a better explanation?'

Stretton let out a sigh.

'I'm not sure what to think,' he replied.

'Whoever it was, I sure aim to find out,' Rimmer said.

He finished the coffee and shifted his position with a groan.

'I guess I owe you an apology,' he said.

'What for?'

'For sendin' you out this way. There's a job to be done, but it was a bad assignment.'

'Lucky you did,' Stretton replied.

Rimmer nodded.

'I don't know why I acted the way I did,' he said. 'I guess it's just that I don't like the way things have been shaping up lately. Trouble is brewin' and some mighty shady characters have suddenly appeared on the scene. I took a look at those 44s of yours and figured you were just another one. I don't hold with gun-slingers.'

'I'm not a gunslinger.'

'Nope, you're probably not.'

The conversation lapsed. Stretton was thinking hard, and when he spoke again it was to raise the issue that had occurred to him.

'If what you say is true,' he said, 'and I've got no reason to doubt it, then it seems to me there could be another reason why you got shot.'

'I don't follow.'

'Someone took a shot at me last night. Maybe that was a coincidence, or maybe someone overheard you giving me orders to come out this way and got here before me. Maybe that bullet was meant for me.'

There was a pause while both men considered the implications of Stretton's words before Rimmer spoke again.

'If you're right, it would mean we've got a spy in the camp.'

'That's the way it seems to me.'

Rimmer grunted.

'It's more likely I was the target,' he said.

'All the same, there's something pretty odd going on. I just don't understand how anyone would know I was even in Buckstrap.'

Rimmer gave Stretton a quizzical look.

'You know what this means?' he said.

Stretton's expression was blank.

'If someone is out to get you, you ain't safe anywhere. So far he's missed out twice. He won't be likely to rest till he's succeeded.'

Rimmer considered his words.

'I suppose you've got a point,' he said.

'Have you any idea who it might be?'

Stretton's expression was grim as he replied.

'As a matter of fact, I do. I came here looking for a man named Yoakum. Seems like he's been taken on by the Bar Seven.'

'Taken on?'

'Yoakum really is a gunslinger. He killed a friend of mine back Texas way.'

'Is that why you're here? To gain revenge?'

'Somethin' like that,' Stretton replied.

Rimmer attempted something resembling a grin.

'Thanks a lot for gettin' me involved. If I took a bullet that was meant for you, then you owe me.'

He sank back against the blanket and closed his eyes. Stretton rolled himself another smoke but when he offered the makings to Rimmer, he realized that the foreman had lapsed into sleep. He got to his feet, made his way to the sorrel, and swung into the saddle. He took out the binoculars and swept the horizon, looking for Rimmer's horse. He spotted it, largely obscured behind some bushes. He put the field glasses back, and then, with a glance at the recumbent form of Rimmer, set off to retrieve it. One way and another, he needed to get Rimmer back to the ranch-house. The foreman had put a brave face on his injury, but he was clearly in pain and needed more assistance than he was able to provide. Beyond that immediate necessity he couldn't think.

3

The Bar Seven lay basking in the noonday heat when a lone horseman rode into the yard. As he dismounted the ranch-house door opened and a man appeared on the veranda.

'Tuplin, you're back,' he said. 'I hope you bring good news.'

'You don't have to worry, Mr Claridge,' the man replied. 'I don't think you'll be having any more trouble from Stretton.'

'Come inside. Leave Rawlins to stable the horse.'

Claridge went back inside and the rider followed him. He was surprised to see that Claridge was not alone. A woman wearing a riding habit was sitting on a settee with a glass in her hand.

'I guess you could do with a drink,' Claridge said, motioning the newcomer to a chair. He went over to a cabinet with an array of bottles and poured a whiskey.

'I think you know Miss Flushing,' he said.

Lana smiled.

'I believe I've seen you from time to time in the Eagle,' she said. The man was clearly uncomfortable. He shifted a little in his seat.

'As you know, Miss Flushing is the proprietor,' Claridge added. 'It rightly deserves the reputation of being the best establishment in town.'

Tuplin swallowed a mouthful of the liquor. He looked uncertainly from Claridge to Lana.

'It's quite all right,' Claridge said. 'Miss Flushing is an old friend of mine. You can speak quite freely.'

The man licked his lips.

'Well,' he said, 'it's like this. After the initial failure to deal with Stretton . . . '

'After your initial failure,' Claridge interposed.

'As you say, Mr Claridge. After my initial failure, I returned to the Sawtooth. You won't believe this, but guess who turned up there today?'

'Don't talk in riddles. Just get on with it.'

'Sorry, Mr Claridge. Well, it was Stretton. I thought at first he was there because he might have spotted me, but then I saw sense. There was no way he could have done so. It was dark and . . .'

'Get on with it.'

'Well, it seems like he was taken on as a hand. But that ain't the best of it. I overheard Rimmer, the ramrod, give him instructions for what to do the next morning. He was sending him right to the boundary fence. I know something of the Sawtooth spread so I made sure I was there waiting for him.'

'And did he show up?'

'He sure did. I got him plumb. Like I say, you won't be having any trouble from him now.'

'Are you sure?'

'Sure I'm sure. I made no mistake this time.'

Claridge turned to Lana.

'Are you all right?' he said. 'You look a little pale.'

She summoned a faint smile.

'I'm fine,' she replied. She turned to Tuplin.

'Speak plainly. Do you mean you killed Stretton?'

'Stone cold,' he replied.

'Well, there you are,' Claridge said. 'I'd heard something about Stretton even before our man Yoakum spilled the beans. Seems like he has something of a reputation. He might have turned the tables back in the Big Bend country, but he isn't going to present a problem here.'

Lana took a sip of her drink.

'I'm not sure I'd believe everything Yoakum has to say,' she remarked.

'I wouldn't put much trust in Yoakum myself, but what he told us about Stretton fits in with what I've heard about him. He's a dangerous man. If he took Lindop's side, it could have made all the difference. And from what Tuplin here has just told us, that's exactly what he appears to have done — even leaving the Yoakum situation out of it.'

He turned back to Tuplin.

'You did a good job this time, and the inside information we're getting is proving very useful. I'll see you get your rewards. Right now, finish your drink and then get on back to the Sawtooth.'

Tuplin didn't need a second invitation. With a confused nod in the direction of Lana, he made for the door and made an awkward exit. When he had gone, Claridge took Lana's glass and refilled it.

'Lana,' he said, 'I think it's time to celebrate.'

He looked at her again.

'Are you sure you feel well?' he said. 'I'd say you were almost shaking.'

'I think I've got a headache coming on,' she replied. 'If you'll excuse me, I think I'll just go and lie down.'

'Of course,' he replied. 'Let me know if there's anything you need.'

She got to her feet and made for the stairs.

'Get better soon,' he added. 'I think this is goin' to be our time.'

There was little conversation between Stretton and Rimmer on the way to the ranch-house. Their only aim was to get Rimmer back so he could see a doctor. They rode steadily so as not to jar the wound unnecessarily, and their slow progress gave Stretton time to speculate on what had happened. The initial hostility between himself and Rimmer seemed to have dissipated. He was pretty sure that Rimmer had been shot in mistake and that he, Stretton, was the intended victim, and as he had told Rimmer, he felt certain he knew who was behind it. It had to be Yoakum. He was the only one with a reason. It certainly seemed that the Sawtooth had been infiltrated by the Bar Seven. Who could have overheard Rimmer? He cast his memory back, but could recall no one else being present at the time Rimmer had given him his instructions. It must have been Yoakum who had taken that first shot at him. His guess was that Yoakum had realized he had been followed even before the encounter in the Eagle Saloon. He might have seen him in the street. Would Yoakum realize he had made a mistake? If and when he did, what would his reaction be?

The ranch-house came into view, and as they approached Lindop himself appeared. He came forward to meet them.

'What happened?' he snapped.

'Rimmer's been shot. Help me get him down.'

Together they half lifted and half carried Rimmer from his horse and into the house, where they laid him on a couch in a room adjoining the main room. Once they were assured he was as comfortable as they could make him, Lindop ordered one of his men to ride into town and get a doctor. Once the sound of his horse's hoofs had faded into the distance, he turned to Stretton.

'I think you'd better explain,' he said.

Stretton outlined the circumstances, keeping his account to a minimum.

When he had finished, he was surprised by Lindop's reaction.

'I just knew it,' he said. 'I've had my suspicions that the Bar Seven were running off cattle, but I couldn't be absolutely sure. Now you tell me that Rimmer has seen Sawtooth stock on Bar Seven range. Well, I ain't gonna stand by and do nothing.'

'There could be some other explanation.'

'What? Rimmer got shot as a result. I reckon if any further proof were needed, then that's it.'

Stretton didn't go into details about what alternative explanation there might be. It was clear that Lindop was convinced that the Bar Seven was responsible for his losses, and that he meant to do something about it. Lindop himself was deep in thought. After a long pause he spoke again.

'I'd like to deal with the Bar Seven right now, but we need to get on with the round-up.' He stopped. His expression was grim.

'I don't know why I'm discussin' this with you,' he said. 'It's Rimmer I should be talkin' to.'

'I can't argue with that.'

'I think that's enough for now,' Lindop said. 'A lot has happened and a lot has been said. You've had a hard time of it today. Get on over to the bunk-house and rest up. The doc should be here soon. One thing seems pretty sure: Rimmer owes the fact that he's still here at all to you. I thank you for that.'

Stretton made for the door. Lindop was right. It had been quite a day and he was feeling tired. He could do with some rest. Once he had recuperated, he might be in a better position to think straight and figure out what needed to be done. When he stepped outside the daylight was beginning to fade. It seemed an awful long time since he had set out early that morning. As he walked towards the bunk-house, he wasn't even thinking about who else might be there and the little matter of unmasking the spy. He was only thinking of sleep.

When Lana had complained to Claridge about having a headache, she hadn't been entirely lying. She genuinely didn't feel so good. She lay for a while on top of the bed while a confused array of thoughts and emotions competed with the pain in her head. Time passed, and she knew it couldn't be long before Claridge came knocking on her door. He had said something about celebrating, and she had a pretty good idea of what that meant. Before he could do so, she raised herself up and sat for a few moments on the side of the bed till her head cleared a little. Then she opened the door and made her way back down the stairs. Claridge was sitting with a drink in his hand and looked up at her approach.

'Are you feeling better?' he asked. Without waiting for a reply he made his way to the drinks cabinet.

'Let me pour you another,' he said.

She made a gesture with her hand.

'Not for me. In fact, I think I'd better be getting on back to town.'

'But the night is young,' Claridge replied. 'Anyway, I thought you'd be staying over.'

'I'd like to,' she answered, 'but I really don't feel quite right.' She smiled. 'I can always come back. Maybe tomorrow.'

'It's getting a bit late. Surely you'd do better to stay right here.'

'I've been spending too many nights away from the Eagle,' she replied. 'I don't like to leave it for too long. Without me there, things are liable to get out of hand.'

Claridge shook his head.

'I don't know why you don't give up that place,' he said. 'Like I've said before, you can move in here any time you like.'

She came up to him and kissed him lightly on the lips.

'Perhaps some day soon,' she said.

She turned and made for the door. After a moment's hesitation Claridge went with her.

'If you're quite determined to leave,' he said, 'I'll walk with you to the stable.'

They didn't say anything while Claridge helped Lana saddle the roan gelding and adjust the stirrups. He didn't like the idea of her leaving, but he knew her well enough not to argue with her. When the horse was ready they embraced and then she swung into the saddle and rode out of the yard. The sun was westering and shadows were beginning to lengthen. She glanced back and Claridge was still standing where she had left him. She rode slowly at first till she was well clear of the ranch-house, and then she touched her spurs to the horse's flanks. It broke into a jog and then a trot, and then picking up more speed, it began to gallop.

Now it was moving fast, and Lana, taking off her hat so that it hung by its strings, allowed her hair to flow out on the wind. The horse was stretching out and she felt a welcome sense of exhilaration. Something tight inside her seemed to loosen. She wasn't sure just what she was doing, but the sense of speed and power helped to relieve some indeterminate sense of pain that she would have been at a loss to put a name to, much less understand. She carried on riding fast and hard for some time until eventually her mood quietened and she slowed the horse down again. She continued riding at a steady pace, and eventually brought the roan to a halt. As the sun sank lower she sat in the saddle, trying to think straight, trying to calm the mix of emotions she felt.

She looked around her, not even sure about where she was going. She had set off with the intention of riding back to town, but something was almost impelling her to ride instead in the direction of the Sawtooth. But what did she expect to find there? Confirmation of what Tuplin had said? She didn't want to believe it, and until she had indisputable proof, she didn't have to. Why should it make such a difference? What was Stretton to her? It was a long time since she had first met him, even before her time with the Mojave. He had obviously no recollection of having seen her before. Maybe the markings on her face made a difference. More likely he had no reason to remember her. She had got over it a long time ago. And then, out of the blue, he had walked into the Eagle saloon.

The questions were ringing in her head. For a few moments she even considered returning to the Bar Seven, but in the end she decided after all to carry on riding to Buckstrap. If a killing had taken place, the news would soon reach town, and one way or the other, she would learn the truth. Either way, she would have a clearer idea of what she should do.

★ ★ ★

Stretton awoke feeling refreshed. Outside the bunk-house there was a trough of water and a piece of glass which acted as a mirror. He plunged his head and neck into the cold water and then

74

shaved as best he could. The air was cool, but it already carried with it a hint of heat to come. When he was ready, he walked over to the ranch-house and knocked on the door. It was opened by Lindop.

'Stretton,' he said. 'Come on in. I figure you could do with some coffee.'

Stretton was thinking he could do with something more substantial, but coffee would do to be going on with. Lindop seemed to be in a better frame of mind. He realized that his new-found affability was owing to the circumstance that Rimmer probably owed his life to him. They went inside and Stretton took a seat while Lindop made for the kitchen. He came out again a few moments later.

'How is Rimmer?' Stretton asked.

Lindop grinned. At that moment an inner door opened and Rimmer himself appeared carrying a tray balanced on one arm.

'See for yourself,' Lindop said. Stretton looked at Rimmer. His arm and shoulder were bandaged and he carried a slight stoop.

'Shouldn't you be restin' up in bed?' Stretton said. He got up and helped Rimmer put the tray down.

'I told you I'd be fine,' Rimmer replied. 'All the doc did was to change the dressings. Looks like you did all the hard work.'

'All the same,' Stretton said, 'maybe you shouldn't be overdoin' it.'

'Stretton's right,' Lindop said, pouring the coffee. 'You don't want to set things back.'

'I figure I'm just about ready to get on a horse again,' Rimmer replied, somewhat irrelevantly. 'Just as soon as I can, I'm goin' after whoever did this to me.'

'You don't know who that is,' Lindop replied.

'I don't, but Stretton does.'

Lindop turned to Stretton.

'Is that right?' he asked. 'How would you know that? Did you see something?'

Stretton took a long drink of coffee before venturing on an explanation, adding little to what he had already said. When he had finished Lindop let out a sigh.

'Are you sure about this man Yoakum?' he asked.

'You're not the first person to ask me that,' Stretton replied. Lindop gave him a curious look, but he didn't elaborate.

'Seems like you got out of the frying pan straight into the fire,' Lindop remarked.

'I don't understand.'

'Well, from what you've said, it looks to me like the situation you were in back in Texas and the situation you find yourself in now are very similar.'

Stretton thought for a moment.

'Yes,' he replied, 'you're right. It's kinda spooky really.'

'Let's hope the outcome's the same,' Rimmer cut in.

Both Lindop and Stretton looked at him questioningly.

'Well, I'm assumin' that the outfit you were ridin' for came out on top,'

Rimmer said to Stretton. 'I guess it did, since you're here.'

'I suppose you could say it did,' Stretton replied. 'It still resulted in some people bein' killed.'

He downed the last of the coffee and got to his feet.

'I'm sure glad to see you lookin' so good,' he said to Rimmer. He turned to Lindop.

'What do you want me to do today?' he asked.

Lindop exchanged a few words with his foreman.

'We've more or less started on the round-up,' Rimmer said. 'How would you feel about helpin' gettin' some of the critters hidin' out in the brush?'

'Brush poppin'. Suits me fine,' Stretton said.

'You'll probably need some assistance. Get Burrage to give you a hand.'

Stretton made his way back to the bunk-house. As he did so, he began to reflect that Burrage could be the informer, but then so could a number of others.

He had racked his brain trying to remember who had been around the evening he had received his orders from Rimmer, but it was to no avail. Burrage turned out to be a comparative youngster, and when they rode out together, Stretton had already forgotten his suspicions.

This time they rode in a different direction, eastwards towards some higher country with a covering of thickets and underbrush. They were riding lightweight horses and carrying short ropes because there would be little room to swing a loop. Because the brush got hot as the day went by, some of the men were already at work, driving the cattle towards whatever natural openings in the brush they could find.

'I figure a moonlight round-up is best,' Stretton remarked.

Burrage nodded in assent. 'Dogs,' he said. 'Dogs are useful.'

The country they were riding was rough with patches of mesquite and prickly pear. They rode into the brush to roust out the cattle, working hard to prevent them circling and getting back in. It was hard, sweaty work but they persisted. A couple of old bulls kept trying to head back for the breaks, but Burrage rode them tight.

'There should be more,' Stretton commented. He remembered what Rimmer had told him about finding rustled cattle on the Bar Seven. 'Too many of those draws are empty.'

As they continued to roust out cattle from the breaks, Burrage proved his worth, dropping a loop each time with great accuracy. Sometimes they worked together and sometimes they split up. By the time they were all ready to call it a day and haze back the animals they had found, their faces were scratched and their outfits were dirty and torn. It had been a hard shift, but Stretton and the younger man had worked well together. Before starting back, Stretton got out the makings and they each rolled a cigarette.

'You're new to the Sawtooth,' Burrage commented.

'Yup. Just started. Seems like I've been here a-whiles already.'

'There was some talk in the bunk-house, somethin' about the ramrod bein' shot.'

Stretton saw no point in being evasive.

'That's right,' he said. 'In fact it was me who found him.'

'Is he going to be OK?'

'He's fine.'

'I guess somethin' like that was bound to happen,' the youngster said. 'It's been brewin'.'

Stretton hadn't intended asking questions, but Burrage seemed willing to talk and it occurred to him it might be a good opportunity to learn more.

'How long have you been with the Sawtooth?' Stretton asked.

'Couple of years. I figure to move on, though, sometime soon. Don't get me wrong. Lindop is a good man to work for, but I figure there's got to be more to life than this.'

'I gather there's trouble between the

Sawtooth and the Bar Seven.'

'Like I said, it's been comin'.'

'Does it worry you?'

'Not too much. In any case, there's nothin' to be done about it.'

Stretton was about to add something but thought better of it. It struck him that if Burrage intended moving on, now might be a good time to do it. But he didn't seem to be thinking that way. That loyalty spoke well for the Sawtooth.

'What if it comes to shooting?' he said. 'That's something you didn't sign up for.'

'I ain't about to run,' the youngster replied.

'How about the others?'

'I'm sure most of 'em would feel the same.'

'Most of them? Not all?'

'I can only speak for myself. You'd have to ask them.'

The conversation slackened while they drew on their cigarettes. Occasionally a bull bellowed and the air was full of the droning of flies.

'There's one or two I wouldn't be so sure about,' Burrage resumed.

'Yeah? Who would they be?'

'There's one *hombre* called Tuplin. I don't know. He hasn't been with the Sawtooth very long and I haven't had a lot of dealin's with him, but I can't seem to get on with him too well.'

'Tuplin you say. Obviously I haven't met him yet.'

'I don't want to speak out of turn. As I say, I don't really know him either. Mr Lindop has been taking on a few new men. Some of them don't look much to me like regular cowpokes.'

Stretton was not carrying his 44s. He wondered if Burrage would have been equally suspicious of him if he had worn them both. He had a sudden uncomfortable feeling. He could carry out the tasks of the ranch as well as the next man, but he was under no illusion that he had been hired for any reason other than his ability with a gun.

'What about the Bar Seven?' he asked.

'What about it?' Burrage replied.

'I gather they've taken over some free range and fenced it in.'

'That don't surprise anyone. Claridge is only able to get away with it because he's got the marshal under his thumb.'

'I thought the Sawtooth was the biggest spread round these parts.'

'Was till now. Claridge, he's the owner of the Bar Seven, has always resented it. He set out to challenge the Sawtooth.'

'And the marshal is on his side?'

'It ain't surprisin'. Apart from anything else, the marshal is his cousin. He don't know nothin' about the law. If there's trouble, he relies on Claridge's men to deal with it.' Stretton was getting more information than he had bargained for. Burrage was waxing quite eloquent. It was as if, once he had got started, he needed to carry on and unburden himself of something. In a moment of inspiration, Stretton thought of Lana.

'What about a lady called Lana Flushing,' he prompted.

'Lana Flushing. She runs the Eagle Saloon. Not that I get in there a lot. Have you met her?'

'Yup.'

'You know she spent some time with the Mojave? The marshal was the one who rescued her. That was a long time ago. He used to be some kind of trader then. Like I said, he's got no qualifications to be a lawman.'

Stretton took a long drag on his cigarette.

'If you don't mind me sayin' so,' he said, 'but you seem to know a lot about this.'

'Not really. It's common knowledge. I only know the bare outlines. In a place like Buckstrap, people get to know one another's business. It would be hard to keep a secret.'

Stretton would have liked to enquire still further into the matter, but there was no more time. The cattle were already on the move and they needed to get back on the job. Without more ado, they climbed into leather and took their places driving the cattle back to the ranch. As he rode, Stretton's mind was occupied with what he had learned. He needed time to sort through it, but one phrase of Burrage's kept recurring: *The marshal was the one who rescued her.* Why did it trouble him? It was the word *rescued*. That didn't tie in with what he remembered of Lana's own description. She had spoken quite favourably of her time with the Mojave. Another thing puzzled him. What was her relation to Claridge? During their conversation she had described him as her friend. Was that just neighbourliness, or something more? And he hadn't forgotten Yoakum. He meant to have revenge, and if anything the issue was even more urgent than before because Yoakum now had another enemy in Rimmer. He meant to get to Yoakum first.

* * *

One person deeply affected by events was Tuplin. He had been totally taken

86

aback when he learned that both Rimmer and Stretton had returned to the Sawtooth, and that Rimmer had been shot. He didn't immediately grasp what must have happened, but when he did he was seized with panic. What remained of his rational faculties told him that he was in no immediate danger, but his every instinct was to flee. One voice told him there was no way he could be associated with the shooting, but another voice told him that the affair would be investigated and that he would emerge as a suspect.

For a brief time he considered fleeing to the Bar Seven, but he quickly realized that he would be even worse off there. Claridge would learn of the affair sooner or later, and once he did, his position would be untenable. He hatched up a wild plot to ride into town and tell the marshal that Stretton had shot Rimmer in order to persuade him to arrest Stretton. He quickly abandoned that idea, too. Finally he decided there was only one thing to do, and that was to make himself scarce.

Without wasting any more time, he saddled up his horse and rode away from the ranch. His instinct was to keep on riding, but he realized that while daylight remained he might be spotted. He didn't take time to reflect that it wouldn't matter, that he had in fact no immediate cause for alarm. He was in a state of funk and could only think of escape. He stopped at the nearest deserted spot where a grove of trees offered cover, and braced himself to wait for nightfall. It was hard to keep patience, and several times he jumped to his feet, thinking that he heard the sound of hoofs, but time slowly passed and darkness finally descended. When he was satisfied that no one would see him, he climbed into the saddle and rode away.

4

A couple of days went by. Stretton and Burrage continued to work as a team alongside some of the other cowboys. They rode into the hills, rounding up wild stock that ranged in the cedar brakes. Some of them were scrawny and in need of fattening up.

'We got a name for some of those critters back in Texas,' Stretton said.

'Yeah? What's that?'

'We call 'em blackjack steers. Ain't too sure just why.'

He wasn't sure either why he had made the remark. He hadn't given much thought to the Big Bend country or to the Hog Eye, and the memory of his friend who had died in the range struggles there was already fading. The round-up was well advanced and they were on to the combings. Stretton appreciated the trust Lindop had placed in them. He knew from experience that the real test of a man on roundup wasn't so much the work done in camp, the roping and branding, but his ability to bring in cattle from the rough country. They were so busy that Tuplin's absence passed unnoticed.

Saturday came round and some of the boys were fixing to go into town. Stretton had volunteered to do some work on the chuck wagon and was busy greasing the axles when Rimmer appeared. His wound had almost healed and he was back to his old self again. Stretton stood up and they shook hands.

'Sure is good to see you back on your feet,' Stretton said.

'Thanks to you,' Rimmer replied.

He paused, looking around him, and then turned back to Stretton.

'You heard about Tuplin?' he said.

'Tuplin?'

'A little weasel. I'd probably have fired him if he hadn't made off himself.'

'Made off?'

'Disappeared. Vamoosed. Gone.'

He paused to let his words sink in. Stretton didn't say anything.

'You know what I think?' Rimmer said. 'I reckon that Tuplin must have been the one who overheard my order to you. I never did trust him. He was always malingerin'. Don't you think it's somethin' of a coincidence? I reckon that once you brought me back to the ranch he got cold feet and skedaddled.'

Stretton was thoughtful.

'That wouldn't be enough reason for him to run off.' He paused.

'Maybe you're right. But then . . . you ain't suggestin' he might have taken that shot at you?'

Rimmer glanced sharply at Stretton.

'You've already told me that this varmint Yoakum was responsible.'

'Yeah. It must have been Youkum,' Stretton replied. 'He's gunnin' for me. It was his mistake.'

His words seemed to hang in the air and there was a moment's silence before Rimmer resumed:

'The boys are plannin' a trip into

town. As ramrod of this outfit, I feel it's my duty to go with them and make sure there's no trouble. Now it occurs to me that Yoakum might be thinkin' of payin' a visit too. Who knows, he might even have Tuplin with him. So how about you stringin' along? It could get mighty interestin'.'

Stretton grinned. 'I think I catch your drift,' he replied.

Rimmer nodded. 'Good. Then it's arranged.' He turned to go, but Stretton caught his arm.

'Yoakum's mine,' he said.

Rimmer burst into a laugh.

'It's me he shot,' he replied. He thought for a moment.

'Let's just see how it plays. If Yoakum is in town, he's likely to have some of his cronies with him. I take it you're not averse to some gun-play, if it should come to that?'

Stretton stroked his chin.

'I reckon not,' he said. 'After all, that's what Lindop hired me for.'

If there was irony in his voice,

Rimmer didn't notice it.

'See you later,' Rimmer replied.

He walked away, and Stretton resumed his task. When he had finished, he didn't go back to the bunkhouse but instead took a walk which led him past the corral and out beyond where most of the cattle were penned. Their pungent smell lay heavy on the air, but it soon grew fainter as he carried on walking till he reached a place where the stream that carried the water supply rippled through a grove of aspens. He lay down in a shady spot and looked up at the sky through a canopy of leaves.

It seemed as though the time was fast approaching when he would achieve his aim and get his revenge on Yoakum. He had expected that he would feel exhilarated, but he didn't feel that way at all. If anything he felt rather flat. His conversation with Rimmer had disturbed him. Maybe he had been working too hard. Maybe he had allowed himself to become distracted. When the time came to strap on his 44s he would feel differently.

Overhead a few flimsy white clouds scudded across the sky. The leaves rustled, and alternate patches of light and shade played upon his upturned features. The water splashed and sparkled, throwing up small amounts of spume and spray where it ran over some rocks. Although the ranch-house was quite close, it seemed as if it were a long way away. He closed his eyes and began to drift into sleep, when suddenly he awoke with a jerk. He got to his feet and quickly made his way back to the bunk-house.

'Where's Burrage?' he barked at the first man he saw.

The man shrugged.

'Never mind,' Stretton said. 'Tell me, did you know someone called Tuplin? He worked here for a time?'

The man grimaced.

'Tuplin? Sure. He didn't exactly endear himself to anyone.'

'Can you describe him.'

'A little runt. Looked like a weasel and acted like one.'

Rimmer had used the same comparison.

'Anything else?' Stretton snapped. 'Why do you want to know?'

'I might have come across him before. Seems like he's lit a shuck. If I'm right, Rimmer could be interested.'

The man shrugged. 'That's about it,' he said. 'I guess you could say he was pretty nondescript.'

'Thanks.'

The man nodded and walked out. Stretton flung himself on his mattress. His head was buzzing, but he set himself to wait till Rimmer returned and it was time to head for town. He had been lying down for only a few minutes when he leaped to his feet and rushed outside. The man he had spoken to was still there.

'Tell me,' he said. 'Have you any idea what kind of horse Tuplin rode?'

'I think it was a grulla,' the man replied. 'Why do you ask?'

'Just curious,' Stretton replied. He returned to the bunkhouse and lay down again. His head still felt muzzy, but he needed to think.

Lana Flushing was right about news getting around. Rumours were rife in the Eagle Saloon. There were different stories, however, so she finally decided to pay a visit on the marshal. As the nominal representative of law and order, he was likely to know the truth of the matter. In addition, the fact that he was in the pay of Claridge and the Bar Seven meant it was even more likely he would know the facts. As she made her way across the main street, she couldn't help feeling nervous. Her throat was tight and her mouth dry. When she entered the marshal's office, she had to make an effort to stay in control.

'Well, good morning,' Malone said. He got to his feet and invited her to take a chair. 'It's sure nice to see you. I take it business is good over at the Eagle?'

'Don't worry,' she replied, 'you'll get your share of the profits.'

'It was Claridge set you up,' he said. 'If there's any concern about profits, he's the one that should worry.'

'Neither he nor you have any cause for concern,' she replied.

'I guess we got off on the wrong foot there somehow,' Malone said. 'I was just makin' small talk. Is there something I can do for you?'

'There are rumours passing around,' she replied. 'From what I can gather, it seems there was some sort of incident at the Sawtooth. Someone got shot.' She paused for a moment. 'Some say it was Lindop's foreman.'

'Then they got it right,' he said.

She swallowed hard and dropped her head.

'Are you OK, Miss Flushing?' Malone said.

She looked him square in the face. 'Sure. I'm fine. I've been a little under the weather, that's all.'

'The way I figure it,' the marshal continued, 'somethin' was bound to happen. Lindop has been pushin' too hard. He's been almost askin' for trouble. I don't figure he's goin' to take this lyin' down.'

'What do you mean?'

'It's been apparent to everyone that the Bar Seven and the Sawtooth can't get along together. A range war has been brewin' for some time. I guess this just brings it one big step nearer.'

For a moment Lana considered telling Malone about Tuplin, but she decided against it. The situation was complicated, and she wasn't sure of how she should react. One thing especially worried her: if Tuplin were responsible, and had shot Rimmer in mistake for Stretton, then what did that say about Yoakum?

'I hope it doesn't come to that,' she said.

The marshal gave her a quizzical look.

'If you don't mind me askin',' he said, 'but why are you interested in what's been happening at the Sawtooth?'

'Isn't that obvious? I run the Eagle. Ranch-hands from both the Bar Seven and the Sawtooth patronize the place. I need to know what's going on, if only to help stop them taking out their differences on the premises.'

Malone considered her words for a moment.

'I guess you're right,' he said. 'Yup, I can see what you're drivin' at.'

She began to rise to her feet. Malone anticipated her by striding to the door and holding it open.

'Thank you,' she said.

He touched the brim of his hat. 'If you have any trouble over there,' he said, 'just send for me.'

'I will,' she replied.

She stepped out into the sunshine. As the door closed behind her she let out a huge sigh of relief. It was with a lighter step that she made her way back towards the Eagle. She knew what her next step should be, and that was to have a word with Yoakum. The only question was whether to ride over to the Bar Seven or wait till he appeared in the saloon. She would normally have wasted no time in making her way to the Bar Seven, but things were different.

In particular, her relationship to Claridge had changed. They had never been close in a romantic sense; it had been more a matter of convenience. He had set her up in business, and she had almost felt as if she owed him something. They had been drawing apart even before the arrival of Stretton; his appearance had simply brought matters to a head. Although she was keen to have a conversation with Yoakum, she decided to wait. In all probability it wouldn't take too long. Yoakum was likely to hit town with some of the other Bar Seven boys on Saturday, if not before. With that reflection her thoughts took another turn. If some of the Sawtooth hands showed up too, things could get hot, and she might need the marshal's assistance.

★ ★ ★

It was late in the day when Tuplin arrived at the trading post by the Locust River. He was relieved to see it, because he had left the Bar Seven in a hurry and was getting very low on provisions. He was also low on funds, but that was not a problem. For a while he sat and observed the scene. He seemed to have come at the right time. The place was quiet. When he was satisfied that he wouldn't be likely to be interrupted, he dug his spurs into the grulla's flanks and rode forwards.

He drew up outside the store, stepped from leather and fastened his horse to the hitching rail. He took a good look all round before stepping through the open door. It took a moment or two for his eyes to adjust. The place was bare except for the supplies, which were piled high and filled some shelves. Behind the counter stood the slightly bent figure of the proprietor.

'Howdy,' he said.

'Howdy,' Tuplin replied.

'Been ridin' far?'

Tuplin didn't reply and the man continued:

'If it's supplies you're needin' you've come to the right place.' He broke into something between a laugh and a cough. 'In fact, it's just about the only place.'

Tuplin took a step forward.

'Guess I'm a little disorganized,' the man said, 'but take your time. Hell, I ain't goin' no place in a hurry.'

Tuplin licked his lips and glanced about him.

'Maybe I can help you?' the man said.

Suddenly Tuplin drew his gun. He turned and fired three times into the man's chest. He reeled backwards, hit the wall behind him, and fell heavily to the ground. Tuplin stepped behind the counter. The man lay with his eyes open, staring at the ceiling while a pool of blood gathered round him. Tuplin stood for a moment, looking at the corpse. He was about to turn away when there was the sound of movement from somewhere within and an elderly woman burst through an inner doorway. She regarded Tuplin with a startled expression before looking down at the floor. She opened her mouth to scream but before she could do so Tuplin fired once more. For a brief moment she continued to regard him before she fell across the body of her husband, blood pumping from her chest.

Tuplin didn't wait. He holstered his gun and then began to rifle through the shelves indiscriminately. His foot slipped as he trod in a pool of blood and he banged his head against the corner of a shelf. He dropped some of the goods and swore loudly before continuing his rampage. With his arms piled high, he finally fled the store. Outside, in the sunlight, he felt exposed and vulnerable. Realizing the futility of trying to carry away the amount he had filched, he flung his burdens to the ground and began to pack his bags with the basics.

As he did so he realized he had left behind some of the things he really needed, and darted back inside the shop. He was getting more and more agitated as he frantically searched for the items he required; he kept glancing at the door, fearful of someone arriving at the store. When his nerves could stand no more, he made his way back outside, jammed the fresh items into his saddle bags, and climbed into the saddle. With a last glance around him, he dug in his spurs and rode away from the trading post.

* ★ ★ ★

Lana Flushing stood at the head of the stairs leading down from her room to the bar of the Eagle Saloon, taking in the scene. In the middle of the room a roulette wheel spun; a couple of men took their places, a pile of celluloid chips stacked beside them in cylinders of red, white and blue. At a table in a corner of the room a game of monte was in progress. No one spoke, but just made signs when they chose to pass, and watched the dealer closely through the haze of tobacco smoke that filled the air. The game started small, but they were soon playing for higher stakes. At the roulette wheel one of the players suddenly let out a wild Rebel yell, having just won on the turn of the wheel. Already things were hotting up. It was time she made her appearance.

As she proceeded down the stairs, the men looked up and there was an appreciable change in the atmosphere. A kind of hush followed the man's shout, and when the noise picked up again, there was a subtle change in tone. She took her place at a corner of the bar.

'How are things?' she asked the bartender.

'The usual Saturday evening,' he replied. 'It's early yet.'

She was feeling a little on edge, and looked up from time to time at the doors. There was no sign yet of Yoakum. The batwings suddenly flew wide and a man she didn't recognize approached the bar.

'Beer,' he said.

The barman poured and the man laid a coin on the counter. He glanced at her and then looked away. The batwings opened again and a group of men came through. She knew most of them. They were from the Sawtooth. She had been too preoccupied with what she might say to Yoakum to give much thought to anything else. Some of the men took a table, while a couple moved to the bar. She was about to say something in the way of greeting when the batwings swung wide once more and another, smaller group of Sawtooth riders entered. Among them was Stretton. Their eyes met, and he briefly stopped in his tracks before stepping forward again. Just ahead of him was the man she recognized as the foreman of the Sawtooth, the man who had been shot. She was disconcerted and couldn't think of his name for a moment, but his presence helped her to regain her composure sufficiently to greet him with a smile.

'Good to see you boys,' she said.

She glanced at Stretton.

'You decided to stay,' she said. It was a statement rather than a question.

Stretton nodded. He was feeling awkward.

'You two acquainted with each other?' Rimmer asked.

'Only slightly,' she replied. There was a brief pause. 'Why don't you take a seat and make yourselves at home? I'll bring over a bottle.'

Rimmer nodded and he and Stretton found a table in a corner near the bar. Stretton sat down and Rimmer took a good look all around to make sure everything was satisfactory with regard to his ranch-hands before he, too, sat down. Things were lively, but seemingly good-natured. Someone had begun playing the piano, but the music was mostly submerged beneath the general hubbub. Some of the Sawtooth men took their places at the gaming tables. After a few moments Lana appeared carrying a tray on which were three glasses and a bottle of bourbon. Stretton reached inside his pocket, but she placed her hand on his arm to stay him.

'This one's on the house,' she said.

'You won't make much profit that way,' Rimmer remarked.

'You don't mind if I join you?' she replied.

Stretton and Rimmer both made to stand up and pull out her chair but she was too quick for them.

'Shall I pour?' she asked.

When she had done so and they had all taken a sip of the whiskey, she turned to Rimmer.

'I heard about what happened,' she said. 'You seem to be making a good recovery.'

'It was thanks to Stretton I'm still alive,' he answered. 'He found me and brought me back in.'

She looked at Stretton.

'It was nothin',' Stretton said.

'Either way, someone is going to pay, and we both know who it is.'

'Yoakum,' Stretton muttered.

Lana took another drink.

'Why not leave it to the marshal?' she asked.

Rimmer laughed. 'The marshal,' he sneered. 'I think we both know where the marshal stands.'

There was a moment's pause before Lana spoke again.

'There something I need to tell you,' she said.

Without warning, from out in the

street, there suddenly arose the sound of gunfire.

'Hell!' Rimmer shouted. 'Looks like somethin's kickin' off.'

He jumped to his feet and began to make for the batwings. Stretton glanced at Lana before following the foreman. They crashed through the batwings together as the shooting rose to a crescendo, some of the other Sawtooth men joining them. They looked up the street from where the gunshots seemed to be coming and heard a rumble of horses' hoofs. Almost enveloped by a cloud of dust, a group of horsemen came galloping into view, firing their six-guns into the air as they came. They rode on, whooping and hollering, as the few people who remained on the streets sought shelter wherever they could, cowering behind stanchions and hiding in doorways. A bullet shattered the windows of a nearby store to smithereens. As they came close, some of the Sawtooth men began to shout:

'It's the Bar Seven boys!'

'Looks like they're on the prod.'

Stretton peered through the cloud of dirt and dust. Riding in the van of the horsemen he recognized Yoakum. He glanced at Rimmer, expecting a reaction, till he remembered that Rimmer didn't know Yoakum — even if he had come across him before in town, there was no way he would recognize him.

The riders began to slow, and finally brought their horses to a halt outside the Eagle Saloon. They continued to shout and a few more shots were fired, but they were more intent now on enjoying the attractions of the Eagle. They spilled from their saddles, barely pausing long enough to tie the horses to the hitching rails before pushing their way inside, some of them exchanging words with the Sawtooth men as they did so.

'Expect they're all gurgle and no guts,' Rimmer remarked. 'Still, I'd better get back in there and keep an eye on things.'

Stretton nodded. 'I'll join you in a moment,' he said.

Rimmer looked at him, but didn't say anything further. He turned and went through the batwings, accompanied by the Sawtooth cowpokes. Stretton remained on the sidewalk, barring the way to the saloon. He had seen his chance. Yoakum had lingered behind the others, taking a last few draws on a cigarette. If he was aware of Stretton's presence, he didn't show it. He finished the cigarette and moved towards the sidewalk. Stretton took a step forward.

'We're startin' to make a habit of this,' he said. 'I guess you didn't even figure I was still around.'

Yoakum looked up and became aware for the first time of who it was confronting him.

'You!' he said.

'You didn't think I was goin' to forget, did you? And now it's not just about Crowther. Now it's personal.'

'I don't know what you're talkin' about.'

'I'm talkin' about Crowther. The man you murdered.'

'I don't know anybody called Crowther.'

'Are you denyin' you rode for the Ox Yoke back in Texas?'

'I ain't denyin' nothin'. Sure I worked for the Ox Yoke. I even remember you. You were ridin' for the Hog Eye. But I don't remember anybody by the name of Crowther.'

Stretton stepped down off the boardwalk.

'I suppose you're denyin' you tried to kill me.'

'Seems to me like it's the other way round.'

'You bushwhacked me right here in town and then you set up an ambush on Sawtooth range. Maybe you don't even realize it, but you got the wrong man. It was Rimmer you shot.'

Yoakum shook his head in exasperation.

'Look, I've got no idea what this is all about. Now are you gonna step aside and let me get to the saloon, or do I have to make you?'

Stretton grinned.

'It's going to have to be the second,' he said.

He took a step away, and they both

began to fan out. A few people who had emerged from their places of hiding now took shelter again and watched proceedings with frightened expressions. An elderly man who had been approaching turned aside and began to walk back the way he had come. For Stretton and Yoakum the noise from the saloon was swallowed by a deeper silence in which they were isolated. Stretton strained his eyes to watch for any change of expression on his opponent's face, but it was hard to see anything clearly. The only real light was that spilling out from the Eagle Saloon. He dropped his gaze to Yoakum's hands which were hovering above his holsters. He knew he was a fast draw.

They had come to a halt. Stretton's senses were strained to a fine point. Now the moment had come, he saw Yoakum large and clear, as though he had moved forward rather than backward. Still he waited. Although he had initiated the confrontation, he wanted Yoakum to make the first move. He was ready. So focused was he that he barely heard the sudden clatter of feet as the batwings swung open, or the voice that cut through the atmosphere like a jagged knife.

'Stop! It wasn't Yoakum who shot Rimmer!'

Yoakum turned and his movement broke the spell. Stretton glanced towards the saloon. A knot of people were milling about on the sidewalk and in the forefront he saw Lana Flushing with Rimmer standing immediately behind her. Before he could do anything, shots suddenly rang out. Someone screamed and he saw Lana fall backwards. People began shouting as bedlam broke out, and the horses tied to the hitching rails reared and whinnied in terror. Forgetting Yoakum, and thinking only of Lana, he rushed forwards. Lana was lying on the sidewalk with one of the Sawtooth men kneeling beside her. Blood was soaking into her dress.

'Stretton,' she breathed.

'Don't talk,' he replied. He looked up. 'Someone get a doctor.'

A crowd of faces peered down at him and he was dimly aware of a smoking gun. Rimmer suddenly appeared.

'Where's Yoakum?' he said.

'He took off somewhere,' a voice replied.

'It's of no importance,' Stretton said.

He turned back to Lana. She gave him a wan smile and then closed her eyes.

'Get her inside!' someone shouted.

'No. Leave her where she is till the doc gets here,' Stretton replied.

He took off his jacket and placed it under her head.

'The rest of you go back in,' Rimmer snapped. 'Give the lady some breathin' space.'

The men began to disperse. When they had done so, Rimmer knelt beside Stretton.

'That varmint,' he said. 'He'll pay for this.'

Stretton thought for a moment.

'It might have been an accident,' he said.

'What do you mean?'

'I mean that Yoakum may not have

been the first person to fire. One of the men had a gun.'

'Naturally. He was protectin' Miss Flushing.'

'Maybe,' Stretton said. 'Let's not jump to conclusions.'

They were silent for a moment. Rimmer stood up again and looked along the main street. A figure appeared carrying a black bag.

'Here comes the doc,' he said.

The doctor was an elderly stooping fellow. He ordered Stretton and Rimmer to stand back and then spent some time bending over Lana's prostrate figure. He pulled apart her dress before opening his bag and beginning to probe and dab at her shoulder. As he was doing so she suddenly let out a loud groan.

'Be careful, doc,' Rimmer said.

She groaned again and then gasped as he continued his ministrations.

'It's a good sign that she's responding.'

'Is she going to be OK?' Stretton asked.

The doctor glanced over his shoulder.

'I think so. There's no real damage. Looks to me like a ricochet.'

He reached up and handed Stretton a bullet.

'.32 calibre. Probably from a Smith & Wesson.'

Stretton put the bullet in his pocket while the doctor finished by binding up Lana's wound.

'Help me get her inside,' he said. He made to put his arms round her shoulders but she shook her head.

'I can manage,' she said.

With a grimace she struggled to her feet.

'Take it steady,' the doctor said. 'We don't want that wound busting open.'

She responded with a wan smile and a glance at Stretton as Rimmer held open the batwings and she walked a little unsteadily inside. A few of the men cheered as she made her way to the bar. She leaned on the counter.

'I sure could use a brandy,' she murmured.

The barman poured and she took a swig before turning to face the room.

'The show's over,' she said. 'Everything's back to normal. Why don't you boys carry on having a good time?'

Stretton glanced around. There was tautness in the atmosphere and a subdued but growing murmur of voices.

'Where's Yoakum?' somebody shouted.

As if in response, a man rose to his feet and walked to the bar where he stood next to Rimmer.

'You heard what Miss Flushing said,' he shouted. 'Don't go concernin' yourself about Yoakum. You came into town to have a good time, so go on and have a good time.'

Stretton guessed he was Rimmer's equivalent, the foreman of the Bar Seven. In any case, his words seemed to have the desired effect. The tension lessened. The men started to return to the gaming tables and the piano began to play. Stretton looked anxiously at Lana. She was putting on a brave show, but the doctor's words had not convinced him. She looked back and their eyes held. It seemed to him that her expression carried a message of reassurance. When she looked away, he was struck by a random thought. Where was the marshal? He might have been expected to put in an appearance. The thought only lasted for a moment. He had more important things on his mind.

5

Stretton was right to wonder about the marshal's absence. There was a reason for it. At that very moment he was in his office with Yoakum. Once he had broken away in the confusion following the shooting outside the Eagle Hotel, Yoakum had made his getaway by slipping down an adjacent alley. He considered himself fortunate to be unhurt. He didn't know who had fired the first shot, but the bullet had passed perilously close to his head.

When he was satisfied he was out of harm's way, he considered what his next move should be. One option was to return to the Eagle and retrieve his horse, but he quickly put that aside as too risky. He could handle Stretton, but it seemed like Rimmer might be out for revenge too. The irony of it was that he didn't know what Stretton was going on about. He had been involved in trouble back in Texas, but he had never heard of anyone called Crowther. He barely knew Stretton. Where had Stretton got the idea he was responsible for Crowther's death — whoever Crowther was? It seemed to him that the safest thing to do would be to find the marshal. Malone was Claridge's friend — they were in cahoots. He could stay with the marshal till things really quieted down, and make his way back to the Bar Seven later.

By keeping to the byways, he managed to circle his way to the marshal's office. He knew the marshal's living quarters were on the floor above, but he didn't have to worry because a light was on in the marshal's office. With a last glance up and down the street to make sure he wasn't being observed, he knocked on the door.

'Who is it?' a voice called.

'It's Yoakum. You remember me? I ride for Claridge and the Bar Seven.'

'The door's open. Come on in.'

When he entered, Malone was sitting on a cane chair with his feet up on the desk. A bottle of whiskey and a glass stood at his elbow, but he made no effort to conceal it.

'I heard shootin',' the marshal said.

'There was a bit of trouble outside the Eagle Saloon. It's settled down now.'

'I was about to go over. What with you and the Sawtooth both hittin' town at the same time, I figured I might be needed at some point.'

Yoakum's eyes fell on the whiskey bottle. Reluctantly the marshal swung his feet off the desk.

'You haven't said what you're doin' here,' he said.

'Just bein' neighbourly. I came in with the boys, but that's about as far as it goes. Let them let off a bit of steam. No harm done. With a man like me, it's different. I don't try to hide what I am. Some punk decides to chance his arm, and then there are consequences.'

'Very thoughtful of you,' the marshal said.

His eyes followed the trajectory of Yoakum's gaze.

'I was just about to have a drink,' he said. 'Care to join me?'

Yoakum grinned.

'Now that's mighty friendly of you,' he said.

Malone produced another glass and poured. They both took a good long swallow.

'That sure hits the spot,' Yoakum remarked. He sat back, already feeling better. They drank some more, and the marshal refilled their glasses.

'Claridge must pay you well,' Malone said.

'Why do you say that?'

'I don't know. I imagine a man in your line isn't goin' to put himself at risk for nothin'.'

Yoakum laughed.

'Hell,' he said, 'it's crazy. It ain't the risk you take that's liable to do for you. I take it that I can talk freely to you?'

'I'm on Claridge's side, if that's what you mean.'

'Then you'll know that he's about ready to take on the Sawtooth.'

'What makes you say that?'

'It's pretty common knowledge around the Bar Seven. Nobody's under any illusions, least of all me. Hell, I know what Claridge hired me for.'

'Just don't talk too loudly about it,' the marshal said. Yoakum glanced at him. He didn't seem to be surprised by what he had told him. Maybe he had reckoned things out for himself. Maybe he figured if there was any trouble, it wouldn't be his concern. How far did his jurisdiction extend?

Yoakum shook his head. 'The point I'm tryin' to make,' he said, 'is that there's no accountin' for things. Take tonight, for instance. I don't know if you've run across a dude by name of Stretton?'

'I think I've come across him.'

'I barely know the man. Seems like he's ridin' for the Sawtooth. Anyway, he seems to hold me responsible for shootin' somebody back in Texas I've never even heard of. I could understand somebody gunnin' for me if they had good cause, but what am I supposed to make of that?'

'It's a mad world.'

'You said it there. That's exactly what it is.'

They stopped talking as the sound of raucous voices and piano music came to their ears from the direction of the Eagle Saloon.

'Anyway, seems like things are back to normal over there,' the marshal said.

★   ★   ★

It was early in the morning and the Eagle Saloon lay in darkness apart from a circle of light cast from a single lamp. Around a table were gathered Lana, Stretton and Rimmer. The rest of the boys from both the Sawtooth and the Bar Seven had left town. Despite the potential for trouble, things had passed off relatively peacefully. Although Rimmer and his counterpart from the Bar Seven had contributed to this, Stretton put it down largely to Lana's influence. Her strength of character was remarkable. He looked at her across the table. She looked pale and her features were drawn, but otherwise she gave no indication that only a few short hours ago she had been shot. She had just told her two companions about Tuplin, and what he had said in her presence on the evening he had turned up at the Bar Seven.

'So Stretton was right when he thought he might have been the intended target?' Rimmer said.

'Yes.'

'But why would Tuplin have wanted to kill Stretton?'

'I can guess the answer to that one,' Stretton said. 'I'm pretty sure that Tuplin is the same man who told me that Yoakum was responsible for shooting my friend Crowther back in Texas. He didn't call himself Tuplin then. He went by the name of Dryden, but it's almost certainly the same man. The way Tuplin's been described to me, it fits.'

'And all the time he was workin' for the Sawtooth, he was really in the pay of the Bar Seven?'

'It looks that way. Not that he was workin' for either of them for very long.'

'Both he and Yoakum arrived at the Bar Seven at the same time, about two months ago.'

'That would tie in with something else. On my way here I called by a trading post on the Locust River. The owner remembered two men stopping by around that time. They match the description of Yoakum and Tuplin.'

'I don't get it,' Rimmer said. 'Why would they be ridin' together, especially if Tuplin had told Stretton that Yoakum was responsible for the killings?'

'I've been thinking about that one,' Stretton said. 'The way I see it is this. Tuplin carried out the killings, but put the blame on Yoakum. Maybe I caught him off guard. He probably figured I'd be out for revenge. When he knew that Yoakum was movin' on, he got nervous. It took some time for me to recover from my own injury. What if I'd figured things out differently during that time? What if I'd picked up some further information putting the blame on him? He decided to get out and persuaded Yoakum to let him ride with him.

'They fetched up here. Both of them got taken on by the Bar Seven, Yoakum for his gunslinging abilities and Tuplin to act as a kind of double agent. When I turned up, Tuplin really did panic. Was I here to get Yoakum, or was it him I was after? He was probably in the saloon the night I met Lana. It was Tuplin who bushwhacked me. That attempt was a failure. When he was on hand to overhear Rimmer giving me my orders, he probably couldn't believe his luck. He knew I was an easy target. The trouble for him was that he mistook Rimmer for me. When he realized his mistake, he lit out.'

Lana and Rimmer exchanged glances.

'The fact that a range war has been brewin' up made it easy for Yoakum and Tuplin to find work,' Rimmer said. He gave Stretton a wry look. 'To be honest, that's why Mr Lindop hired Stretton.'

'He got me wrong,' Stretton said. 'I'm not a gunslinger.'

'It's likely to come to fightin' in any event. None of us might have a choice.'

Following Rimmer's comment, there was a moment of silence. Stretton was thoughtful.

'A lot of folk seem to be blamin' the Sawtooth for most of this,' he said, 'but it seems to me that Claridge don't come out of it any too well.'

Despite himself, he couldn't help looking at Lana.

'You're right,' she replied. 'I don't know what's happened to Claridge these last few months. He's changed.'

She paused, as if searching for the right words.

'You know it was Claridge who set me up here at the Eagle Saloon?'

'Yes,' Rimmer replied. 'Didn't he and the marshal rescue you from the Indians?'

''Rescued' isn't the word I would

use. But you're right. I guess they figured they were doin' the right thing. Anyway, they brought me back here. I was grateful in a way. Claridge and I got on OK. We were on friendly terms. There was a kind of understanding between us. The Bar Seven was someplace I could go. Then, like I say, he began to change. He always took pride in the Bar Seven, but it gradually became more and more necessary to him. What he had didn't seem to be enough any more. He wanted to grow, to acquire more land and to take on the Sawtooth as the biggest spread. I didn't like what was happening. I began to feel uncomfortable when I was with him. I started visiting the Bar Seven less frequently. I didn't like the looks of some of the people he was hiring.' She looked at Stretton. 'Your friend Yoakum was one of them.'

Stretton nodded.

'I could do with having a few words with Yoakum, once he shows up,' he remarked, 'but it isn't important. I think he'd only confirm what we've been sayin'.'

'It would clear up the little matter of who fired the bullet that wounded Miss Flushing.'

'It doesn't matter now,' she said. 'In any case, the doc said it was a ricochet.'

Again there was a silence till Stretton spoke again.

'That leaves Tuplin.'

'It sure does,' Rimmer added.

Lana regarded them both.

'What do you mean?' she asked. 'Surely you don't intend going after him now?'

'That's exactly what I intend doin',' Stretton replied.

Rimmer let out a strangled laugh.

'I think you're forgettin' something,' he said. 'I'm the man he shot.'

'I don't mean to downplay anything.' Stretton replied, 'but that was an accident. And the bullet was meant for me. It was my friend he killed back in Texas. I've come a long way for payback. All right, I had the wrong man. But I don't intend leavin' it now.'

'Maybe so,' Rimmer began, but he didn't get any further. Suddenly there didn't seem to be much point in arguing about the matter, and just at that juncture Lana broke in with a huge sigh.

'What are you talking about? Have you learned nothing? Either of you? What good has all this talk of vengeance done? Both Rimmer and I were almost killed. Isn't that enough?'

'That's even more reason to find Tuplin.'

'Oh, and bring him back to Buckstrap to stand trial? Is that your idea? I don't think so. In fact, can you be sure that Tuplin is your man even now?'

There was no reply. With a final gesture of exasperation Lana rose to her feet and began to make for the stairs.

'Here, let us help you,' Rimmer said.

She glanced back and shook her head.

'It's been a long, long day,' she said. 'You boys can go or stay if you like, but right now I just want to be alone.'

Rimmer and Stretton watched as she reached the stairs.

'Are you sure,' Rimmer began to mumble but she cut him short.

'I can manage. I'll see you around.' She paused for a moment before adding: 'Maybe.'

They continued to watch her as she slowly made her way up the stairs till she disappeared round a bend; then Rimmer turned back to Stretton.

'You really mean to go after Tuplin?' he asked.

Stretton nodded. 'For both our sakes,' he replied.

* * *

Tuplin was a worried man. He thought that by getting away from the Bar Seven he would be safe, but now he wasn't so sure. Stretton, after all, had persisted in trailing Yoakum until he finally caught up with him months after the original incident. When he had told Stretton that Yoakum was responsible for the death of his friend, he had done so partly on the possibility that Stretton would seek revenge. He had his own reasons for wanting Yoakum out of the way. When Yoakum decided to move on, he had chosen to accompany him partly because he was in something of a blue funk about the murder he had committed. What if Yoakum changed his mind and decided not to take him at his word? What if he decided to investigate the murder a little more closely? What if the truth got out some other way? It seemed wise to make his exit along with Yoakum. The fact that Yoakum was leaving was a good pretext for him to do likewise.

It only occurred to him later that it might be sensible to keep tabs on Yoakum. If he was somehow to find out that he had put the blame for the killing on him, it wouldn't augur too well for his well-being. In the end he had decided the safest thing would be to get rid of Yoakum. Stretton would get the blame, and there would be no reason for anyone to suspect him. Well, it hadn't turned out that way. In fact, he was beginning to wonder whether it had been wise to run away from the Bar Seven at all. There was still no reason why he should come under particular suspicion. The truth was he had panicked, the same way he had done in the past. But it was no use regretting things. He needed to decide where he was going next. His first inclination had been to make his way back to Texas, but now he was doubtful. He would be returning to the situation from which he had fled in the first place.

All these thoughts were ringing in his head as he rode away from the trading post, but he hadn't gone too far when he brought his horse to a halt. For a considerable length of time he sat there, pondering. Should he continue all the way to Texas? Or should he try something new? Gradually he lifted his gaze towards the hills. He would be safe there. No one would expect him to head for the high country. But why think along those lines? Nobody was coming after him. Nobody was trailing him. He was allowing his vague fears to get the better of him. All the same, it made sense. He didn't have to stay long. He could even . . . his thoughts came to a halt. There was another answer. There was a comfortable place ready for him that was already supplied with everything he might need: the trading post.

He had been a fool not to think of it in the first place. With just a minimum of luck he could get back in time before anybody found out what had happened. He could remove the bodies and any traces of the violence that had occurred and set himself up. The store didn't seem to have a lot of customers. If anybody asked, he could just say the former proprietors had sold out and moved on, and that he was the new owner. It seemed an attractive proposition, and he had turned his horse round and was already on the way back when he had second thoughts. It was too risky. He didn't know how many customers the trading post had, but even if they were few in number, somebody would be bound to become suspicious. He wasn't sure he had the nerve to carry it off. And what did he know about keeping a store?

There was another reason which he wouldn't admit even to himself. He had no scruples about shooting somebody down in cold blood, but it was a different matter living next to their corpses. He was superstitious. They might come back to haunt him. He wasn't sure his nerves would be up to it, how he would react when the wind blew about the cabin and the stair treads creaked. No, the trading post maybe wasn't such a good idea after all. The hills offered a better prospect, at least in the short term. When sufficient time had passed for him to feel confident he was safe, he would be ready to move on.

* * *

Back at the Sawtooth, the cattle had been brought together and gathered in the corrals where they had been left without food or water for a couple of days to tame them down. When the time came to release them, they would not immediately stampede into the brush. Lindop, standing beside Rimmer, regarded them with a practised eye.

'Seems to me it's a pity we can't work with the Bar Seven, same as some of the neighbouring spreads,' Rimmer said. 'It would make things simple.'

'You and I both know that ain't nothin' but a pipedream,' Lindop replied. 'The way things are, we'll be lucky to ever get started.'

'What do you mean?'

'I mean that all the bad feelin' between the Sawtooth and the Bar Seven is likely to spill over at any time into a real shootin' war. We were fortunate things didn't boil over the other night at the Eagle Saloon.'

'Miss Flushing might not agree with you there.'

'Don't get me wrong. Miss Flushing was plumb unlucky to take a bullet, but it could have been much worse. In the end, it was largely down to her that matters didn't get completely out of hand. That's quite a lady.'

'I take your point, though,' Rimmer said. 'The quicker we get those beefs on the hoof the better.'

Rimmer, too, knew the importance of the trail drive. He had sat with Lindop late into the night working out the financial details of the drive, and the margins were tight. Now that the cattle had been rounded up, there was no point in delay.

'I'll get the men to cut out their horses,' he said.

He turned and began to walk away in the direction of the corrals. A number of horses had been added to the remuda, so they were fairly full. He stood for a while, regarding them, before turning on his heels and making his way to the stable building where his old lariat was still stored. He picked it up and hefted it with pleasure. It was made of braided cotton, not rawhide.

Returning to the corrals, he picked out a dun, took a moment to figure the direction of the breeze and the distance between him and the horse, then swung the loop and let it go with one quick movement of his right arm. The rope sailed over the heads of a dozen intervening horses and landed neatly over the dun's head. He braced himself for any reaction, but the horse was obviously used to the rope and there was none. He entered the corral and walked up to it with a smile on his lips.

Although his action had been a little extravagant, he had picked out his first mount for the trail drive, and he felt better than he had for some time. Things had not been so good round the ranch for a long while. It would be a relief to be on the trail, to forget for a while all the troubles and intrigues. Strangely, he no longer felt any desire to get even with the man who had shot him. Now he was the trail boss, other things seemed less important. He was no longer in competition with Stretton about who should have priority in meting out justice. He was content to leave that to him. Maybe after he had been on the trail for a few days or a few weeks, he might feel differently too.

* * *

Stretton had not long returned to the bunk-house when Rimmer came through the door.

'Hello,' he said. 'I hoped I might catch you.'

'Why is that? You got something for me to do?'

'Nope, I just happened to be thinkin' of you.'

'I'm not sure that's a good thing or a bad,' Stretton replied.

Rimmer sat down on the edge of the bunk.

'I guess that kinda depends. Are you still thinkin' of goin' after Tuplin?'

Stretton nodded. 'I sure am,' he said.

'You know we're startin' on the trail drive real soon?'

Stretton didn't reply and Rimmer looked up sharply.

'I think you're probably makin' a mistake,' he said, 'but that's your business. Either way, you're goin' to have to put it to one side for a while.'

'No, I'm not,' Stretton said.

Rimmer looked closely at his friend.

'What do you mean?' he asked. 'Like I said, we'll be startin' the herd in another day or two.'

'Then you'll have to start without me,' Stretton replied.

'We ain't carryin' any passengers,' Rimmer said. 'We're gonna need every man we've got.'

'You'll manage without me. You were doin' fine before ever I arrived.'

Rimmer opened his mouth to reply, but then closed it again. For a few moments he seemed to be struggling with himself to find the right words to say. Finally he got to his feet again.

'You can't just walk out on us,' he said. 'You'd be no better than Tuplin.'

'Don't say that,' Stretton snapped.

'Why not? It's true, isn't it? That's just what Tuplin did.'

'It ain't the same thing.'

'So, you've decided that goin' after Tuplin is more important than fulfillin' your duties to the Sawtooth? You signed up with the outfit. You owe it.'

'It's no use you tryin' to persuade me to stay. I'll carry out my duties. I'll stand by the Sawtooth. Just give me a few days. I'll catch up with Tuplin soon enough. If you can't give me the time, if you really have to get goin' as quick as you say, then I'll get back just as fast as I can. You won't have gone far. I'll work all the harder to make up for any time I've lost.'

Rimmer grunted.

'You say that,' he replied, 'but you don't know how long it will take to catch up with Tuplin. Maybe you won't catch up with him. He's got a good start on you. His trail won't be easy to find.'

'I'll find it.'

'Why not wait? You've waited already.'

'Too long,' Stretton said. 'I was plumb lucky to find him here. If I waited till the cattle drive is over, his trail really would have gone cold.'

Rimmer stared hard at Stretton.

'I can't persuade you, can I?' he said.

Stretton shook his head.

'I don't agree with what you're doin'. And I don't know if Lindop would even want you back again.'

Stretton shrugged.

'That's Lindop's affair,' he said. 'I'll be back as soon as I can. That's all I can say. If it's not enough . . . '

His voice trailed away. Rimmer regarded him closely once more, and then moved to the bunk-house door.

'I owe you my life,' he said. 'Nothin' changes that.'

He turned and went out, leaving the door open. Stretton stood still, watching the empty door-frame for a long time before finally turning away and unhitching his gun-belt from where it hung from a nail in the bunk-house wall.

★ ★ ★

When Yoakum got back to the Bar Seven on the morning following his conversation with the marshal, it was to find the place abuzz with excitement. After the previous night's events, he had expected things to be quiet because the boys had expended their energies in town, but the atmosphere was quite otherwise. The reason soon became obvious when he strode into the bunk-house.

'Where have you been, Yoakum?' one of the men asked.

'I had some business in town.'

His words were met by guffaws of laughter.

'What kind of business?' a voice yelled.

'I think we can guess,' another man called.

Yoakum didn't rise to their promptings and the ribbing soon died down.

'Why aren't you boys out on the range?' he asked.

For a moment the laughter was renewed, and then one of the men approached him.

'I guess you haven't heard,' he said. 'We're ridin' against the Sawtooth.'

Yoakum looked hard at him.

'You'd better explain?' he said.

'There's nothin' to explain. It's just like I said. The boss has decided there's been enough pussyfootin'. The time has come for action.'

'He's just not long told us the score,' another man put in. 'Guess you'll be puttin' those guns to good use.'

'When?' Yoakum said.

'Any time soon. Seems like Lindop's herd is trail ready. Once they're on the move, that's when we hit 'em.'

Yoakum's thoughts went back to the marshal's attitude the previous night. His lack of interest made more sense now. It seemed like he had already been informed of Claridge's intentions.

'That's good news,' he said. 'I've been gettin' tired of hangin' about doin' nothin'.'

146

There was a moment's pause and then somebody let out a whoop. Other voices joined in. Yoakum himself didn't feel quite as enthused, but the general excitement was infectious and he found himself being drawn in. After a time, too, he remembered what had happened with Stretton. Stretton was a dangerous man, and he would feel safer without him around. The apparently imminent conflict would provide him with the occasion to get him off his back.

'The Sawtooth has been askin' for it!' he exclaimed. 'And now they're goin' to get it!'

6

It was still dark when Stretton rode away from the Sawtooth. He had little hope of being able to find Tuplin's trail, but he had a pretty good idea about which direction he would go. To the west lay the badlands. Tuplin would naturally head east, towards the Locust River, beyond which lay country with which he was more familiar. He had come that way previously with Yoakum. Chances were that he would stop by the trading post for supplies.

As he rode, Stretton had to fight a strong inclination to head for Buckstrap. Since the evening she had been shot he had not heard from Lana. It wasn't that he was too concerned about her health: she was a strong woman, and he had no doubt but that she would make a complete recovery. It was more a desire just to see her, coupled with a need to justify himself. Their previous meeting, when he and Rimmer had spoken together with her, had ended on an unsatisfactory note. Things had been left hanging in the air. Words had been spoken which hadn't conveyed quite what they were meant to say, and other words had remained unspoken.

Without openly condemning his attitude, she had managed to convey a sense of disapproval. He needed to explain himself, to express his feelings, but at the same time he wasn't clear what his feelings were himself. They were complicated; in essence, what he wanted was her. At the same time he felt afraid — afraid that she might have turned away from him, afraid that he might not be able to resist her if she tried to persuade him to do anything other than what he intended. His mind was in a jumble. Finally he evaded the issue by reflecting that it was too early, that the town would still be asleep. Instead he tried to concentrate his thoughts on the job in hand. The immediate task was to find Tuplin, and find him as quickly as possible.

He rode steadily, allowing the sorrel to pick its own easy pace. Apart from any other consideration, he didn't want it stumbling over some object in the darkness or putting its hoof into a prairie dog hole. The first glow of dawn began to tinge the sky, and he was struck by the emptiness of the land. He didn't realize at first why this was the case, till he remembered that the cattle had all been rounded up. Rimmer would soon be on his way. He had a momentary stab of regret that he wouldn't be with him, and to assuage the sensation he began to reason with himself. He had no intention of avoiding the cattle drive. He might miss out on the first day or two, but it wouldn't take him long to find Tuplin, and once he had dealt with him, he would be right back. He would offer his services even if Lindop refused to pay him. He would more than make up for any time lost.

All the same, he felt uneasy, and when he arrived at the junction of a narrow side trail which he knew led in the direction of town, he was torn once again by the desire to see Lana. It was light now. Day had broken. The town would soon be about its business so his earlier excuse was irrelevant. He brought his horse to a halt and sat indecisively for a few moments before finally moving on again.

★   ★   ★

Rimmer wasn't sure just exactly when Stretton had left. He still entertained some hope that he might change his mind and stay with the trail drive, but when the morning dawned and they were ready to ride, there was no sign of him. Rimmer put the whole matter out of his mind. As trail boss, he had plenty of other things to think about. Starting out usually involved a certain amount of confusion, and the cattle were likely to give trouble till they became used to travelling. He intended driving them hard for the first couple of days in order to tire them. The herd was strung out for three quarters of a mile, the point men riding out and back from the lead cattle but closing in occasionally, the swing men seeing that none of the cattle wandered off or dropped out. They travelled slowly. Towards noon the cattle were halted and allowed to graze. Rimmer wanted to push them on fast, however, so before long they were on the trail once more.

The afternoon passed and it was approaching dark. Riding ahead, Rimmer found a good place with plenty of grass and water to bed the cattle down, and he gave the order for them to stop and the cattle to be grazed. While they did so, the men ate.

As the sun began to sink in the west, they started to work the cattle into a tighter space till soon they were all bedded down in a circle. They had to be watched throughout the night, and the men took it in turns to do a shift of about two hours. Rimmer himself took the cocktail watch, the last watch before daylight. He turned in comparatively early, but found it hard to sleep. For the first time since the morning he thought about Stretton. Where was he now? He would have done better to ride with the trail drive.

He slumbered, and when he awoke the eastern sky was already beginning to lighten. He saddled his horse and climbed into leather. He began his circuit of the herd, and before the watch was over it was morning and the cattle were beginning to stir. He made his way to the chuck wagon. The chef had cooked up a breakfast of sourdough biscuits baked in his Dutch oven, with meat and gravy. While he ate he was thinking of the day ahead. The herd was already beginning to organize itself and take shape, with the stronger cattle in the lead and the weaker ones in the drag. Once the last watch was relieved, the cattle were put in motion.

'Head 'em up and string 'em out!' Rimmer called.

As the cattle passed, he and another man took their places on either side of the column of beasts and began counting them. Their forefingers rose and fell, and when they reached a hundred each of them dropped a pebble into his pocket. When the herd had passed and they counted their tally, they checked. Rimmer rode to the front of the herd and so another day began. It passed much like the first, and night was beginning to fall when the cattle were put on the next bedding ground. Rimmer was satisfied. They were making steady progress. The chuck wagon tongue was pointed in the direction to be travelled the next day, and inside the wagon sheet hung a lantern as a beacon in the darkness.

★ ★ ★

Claridge and his men were in high spirits as they rode out of the Bar Seven. They continued that way till they began to get near to the Sawtooth, when he ordered them to be quiet. As he had anticipated, they had met with no opposition after entering Sawtooth property. Most of Lindop's crew were with the trail drive. It was fair to assume that he had only left a few behind. After all, he had no reason to expect an out-and-out assault on the Sawtooth. It was going to be easy taking the place over, and once he had done so he would proceed to attack and seize the herd.

They rode on and presently came within sight of the Sawtooth. The place was still and the corrals were empty. Claridge took out his field glasses to take a closer look.

'There's nobody about,' he said to his foreman.

'We sure didn't see anybody ridin' in.'

They continued to sit their horses and observe the scene. Presently a figure emerged from one of the barns and made its way to the ranch-house. It paused for a moment on the veranda, and then went inside. Claridge continued to wait.

'How long do you aim to sit here?'

the foreman asked.

'Just as long as it takes,' Claridge replied.

'Why don't we ride right on down?'

Claridge took another look all around.

'There's no point in takin' any chances,' he said. 'We might have been seen on the way in.'

He waited a while longer and then came to a decision.

'This is the way I figure it,' he said. 'Just in case there's any resistance, we'll place some of the men so we've got the ranch surrounded.'

The foreman shrugged.

'OK men,' he shouted. 'You heard what Mr Claridge said. Leave the horses here. Some of you spread out.'

'If any shootin's required,' Claridge said, 'wait till I give the signal.'

When he was satisfied that the men were in position and knew their roles, he looked around at the remaining horsemen.

'Everyone ready?' he asked.

The men nodded in confirmation.

'Sure. Let's go get the varmints.'

Without more ado, Claridge spurred his horse. He and his men began to move towards the ranch-house. Claridge's eyes flickered from one building to another, but the foreman's eyes were fixed straight ahead on the ranch-house. He was looking for any sign of trouble; a glint of light on a gun barrel, the twitch of a curtain. He considered Claridge was being too cautious. The distance between them and the ranch-house diminished and they rode into the yard without incident. As Claridge dismounted, the door of the ranch-house was flung open and the man they had seen previously appeared on the veranda.

'Claridge,' he said. 'What are you and your boys doin' here?'

He looked at the Bar Seven riders. Their rifles were in their hands. Claridge stepped forward.

'We don't want any trouble,' he said.

'Looks like you've brought it,' the man replied.

'I won't beat about the bush,' Claridge said. 'The fact of the matter is,

I'm taking over the Sawtooth. As you can see, resistance would be useless. So I advise you to accept the situation and not attempt any heroics.'

'What do you mean, you're taking over the Sawtooth?'

'Just exactly what I say. It won't make any difference to you. I'm gonna need men. You won't lose your jobs. You'll be kept on and you won't even notice the difference.'

The man looked again at the horsemen. He seemed uncertain what to do, but the decision was taken out of his hands. Suddenly, from the direction of the stables, a shot rent the air. Instantly the scene changed. The man ducked back through the door as Claridge sprang on to his horse. The bunched horsemen split apart and began to ride in different directions as more shots rang out.

Screened by some bushes, Yoakum watched the proceedings. Once the first shot was fired, there was no need for Claridge's signal. As the horsemen scattered, he raised his rifle and opened fire, aiming at the puffs of smoke that were now issuing from the stables. Bullets began to whine over his head, and he continued pumping lead till his rifle was empty. He jerked more bullets into the chamber and started to fire again. He saw a figure emerge from the back of the ranch-house, running towards the stables, and took aim. He squeezed the trigger and the man staggered before continuing his run. A regular fusillade of shots was pouring down on the ranch-house, but there didn't seem to be much in the way of reply. He glanced about him, but was instantly jerked back to attention by a burst of shooting from the outbuildings.

Suddenly, from the stables, three horse-men emerged, riding hard and bending low over their saddles. He squeezed the trigger of his Winchester and one of the horses went down, throwing its rider. Another man fell backwards and was dragged along behind his galloping horse. It was hard to keep track of what was happening. There was one horseman left and as he sped away, he was being followed by some of the Bar Seven men. A man appeared, running hard, before disappearing around the corner of a building. Presently the sound of hoofbeats indicated he had got away. Meantime, the shooting had ceased.

He waited for a few moments, listening to the silence till, after a short time, he heard voices. Men began to emerge from cover, and then Claridge himself appeared. For a few moments nobody spoke. They were still feeling nervous, not yet convinced that they had carried the day. A few of them began to move gingerly towards the ranchhouse. Very cautiously the foreman climbed the steps to the veranda and stood outside. He signalled to Yoakum, who came forward and pressed his shoulder against the door. It flew open and the foreman rushed inside, followed by a few others. They glanced around, their guns at the ready, but there was no sign of anybody. Quickly they fanned out and began to search through the rooms. The place was empty. Obviously the man who had come out to parley with Claridge was the only inhabitant, and he had made good his getaway. The ranch had been only lightly defended. Claridge appeared as his men gathered in the main room.

'Well,' he said, 'I think we can now safely say that the Sawtooth belongs to us.'

Instantly the men began to cheer; one of them fired his six-gun, and a chandelier came crashing down. The noise seemed to sober them, and the man quickly holstered the offending weapon. A few more of Claridge's men came though the door.

'Thanks to you all, every one of you,' Claridge said. 'Make yourselves at home. There's celebratin' to be done!'

* * *

Stretton was approaching the Locust River trading post. He was feeling a little apprehensive, because he would soon find out whether his surmise had been correct or not. If he was right, and Tuplin had come that way, it would be confirmed and he should be able to pick up some information. If not, he was back to square one and Tuplin could be anywhere. He had moments of doubt. Maybe Tuplin had made for the badlands after all. From the point of view of possible pursuit, that would have been the safer option. Maybe he had headed somewhere else altogether. Well, he would soon find out.

He crested a small rise and came within sight of the river and the trading post. Instantly he knew that something was wrong. Horses were tied to the hitch rails and a little knot of people was standing beside a mound at a little distance from the building. Some of them were carrying spades. Among them he recognized the man who had been there with the proprietor on his first visit. The others comprised a motley crew. They looked up at his approach, some of them shielding their eyes against the sun. Two of them drew their guns. When he was close to them, he got down from the saddle.

'What's goin' on?' he said.

One of the men, with lank dark hair gathered in a pigtail, stepped forwards.

'Perhaps you'd better say who you are, stranger,' he replied.

'The name's Stretton and I'm passin' through. I figured to pick up some supplies.'

'You ain't got no pack horse.'

'I didn't figure bein' long on the trail.'

The two men who had drawn their guns moved towards him and Stretton was preparing for trouble when a voice called out:

'He's OK. I've seen him before.'

A man came forwards and looked more closely at Stretton.

'Ain't you the feller came by a few weeks ago askin' about some *hombre*?'

Stretton recognized him as the man who had been with the proprietor of the store when he came by the first time.

'Yeah, that's me. I remember you.' He drew his hand across his brow. 'Ain't no breeze today either.'

163

The man turned to the two with the guns in their hands.

'You can put 'em away,' he said.

They exchanged glances with each other and then, after giving Stretton another glance, placed their firearms back in their holsters.

'What's happenin' here?' Stretton asked.

'Can't you guess?'

'I can guess but I'd like to know.'

'We just buried old Bob Johnston and his wife. Somebody murdered them. In cold blood.'

'How do you know?'

'I don't figure you. What do you mean, how do we know?'

'That it was cold-blooded murder.'

'When you find two bodies each with a gaping wound just oozing blood and neither of 'em carryin' arms, I think it's pretty obvious. Besides, Johnston was a peaceable man. He ain't ever had an argument with anyone.'

The man who Stretton had previously met gave him a quizzical look.

'What are you doin' back here? Last

time you were on the trail of someone. Did you find him?'

'I found who I was lookin' for,' Stretton replied. 'Now I'm on the trail of somebody else.'

'Seems like you spend a lot of time searchin' for people. What are you? Some kind of bounty hunter?'

Stretton ignored the remark. Instead he answered with a question of his own.

'As I recall, when I made enquiries last time, you mentioned that two men had stopped by. You described one of 'em as small and runtish. You said that for some reason you didn't take to him.'

'Maybe I did. So what?'

'Have you seen him again? Recently.'

He was about to reply when the man with the pigtail suddenly intervened.

'Why are you askin' so many questions?'

Stretton paused before replying.

'Because I have reason to believe the man I'm askin' about might be the one responsible for killing your friend Johnston and his wife.'

His words had the desired effect. A

look of surprise spread over the man's features and a few of the others let out a gasp. From the back of the group another person emerged.

'I saw someone. Just yesterday. I was makin' for the store. He passed me. He was kinda small. I greeted him, but he just rode on by. There was something about him . . . '

'What kind of horse was he ridin'?'

'A grulla.'

'Which way was he headin?'

'Towards the hills.'

Stretton's eyes wandered to the distant peaks.

'Is there anythin' up there?' he asked.

'Nope. Some prospectors set up a camp there one time, but they didn't find anythin'. That's when the tradin' post got started. When they left, old Johnston found it hard to make a livin'. It was us few farmers that kept him goin'.'

'We're gonna have to look somewhere else for our supplies now,' a voice commented.

Stretton stroked his chin. He was

considering what he had been told. Could the man who had been seen riding towards the hills be Tuplin? On the face of it, it didn't seem likely. He would have expected Tuplin to keep on going, maybe all the way back to Texas. On the other hand, the description of both man and horse seemed to fit. If it was Tuplin, he wasn't very far ahead. He had made up a lot of ground. Maybe Tuplin had wavered and spent longer getting to the Locust River. All in all, following the lead he had been given seemed the best thing to do. He turned to his informant.

'Is there anything else you can tell me about the man you saw?' he said.

The man shook his head. 'Sorry. I didn't think anythin' of it till now.'

The man with the long braid looked closely at Stretton.

'Are you figurin' to go after the varmint?' he asked.

Stretton nodded. 'Yes, I am,' he replied. He glanced in the direction of the store.

'I reckon there are a few things I might need,' he said.

'You might as well take what you want,' someone replied.

'I won't do that,' Stretton said.

A few of the men had picked up their spades and begun to make their way towards the store. The rest started to follow.

'You might have some hard ridin' to do,' the braided man said. 'I figure your horse could do with some feedin'.'

'Appreciate it,' Stretton said.

He began to move in the direction of the store when the man stopped him by placing a hand on his arm.

'Whatever you have against this man ain't any of my business, but you're also actin' for us now. Johnston was a good friend of mine, a good friend to all of us. Make sure you get the varmint.'

★　★　★

It was a cloudy night, dark and humid. Rimmer reckoned there would be rain,

168

and presently it began to fall, slowly at first but increasing to a steady downpour. The wind blew up, and towards dawn, as the rain drove in, there was a danger that the horses might scatter, so Rimmer helped the wrangler bring them in.

Breakfast was a miserable affair. The cattle seemed to feel the same way, being sullen and reluctant to leave the bedding ground. Once they were put on the move, they were nervous and the men had to work hard to keep them from straying. The storm raged all morning, but towards noon it began to abate and the herd was allowed to graze. Riding was difficult, and the wind blew the rain in squalls. When they eventually continued on their way, they did not cover much ground. Despite his intention of keeping them moving, it wasn't long before Rimmer decided it might be a good idea to bed the cattle down. They proved malleable and the task was achieved with relative ease. Then the night herders took up their posts, while those not on duty slept with their ears to the ground, awaiting their turn.

★ ★ ★

Stretton found no difficulty in following the trail which led into the hills. The ford across the Locust River was signposted from the trading post, and after a time he arrived on the river bank. At some point there must also have been a ferry; the remnants of what had once been a landing stage still remained, its wooden posts and timbers sagging into the water. Gently he encouraged his horse into the river. The water was higher than he had anticipated, and came lapping over his boots and up the sorrel's flanks. He could feel the animal straining against the pull of the current as the water rose still higher. Any deeper and the horse would have to start swimming, but he was past the middle now and after a few more paces the water began to recede as the sorrel emerged dripping on the further bank. He stopped for a few minutes to let it recover before starting forward again.

He hadn't gone very far when he found horse droppings. Since it was unlikely anybody had ridden that way recently, he guessed they had been made by Tuplin's grulla. It was the first real sign that he was on the right track and no longer relying on guesswork, unless the man who had been seen heading in the direction of the hills was not Tuplin after all. Maybe he was getting it all wrong. Still, it was an encouraging sign. The hills were not empty.

The path led him steadily upwards, and he was careful to let the horse choose its way. As he ascended, the air grew cooler. At a turn in the trail he lost sight of the river, and then it reappeared like a green snake beneath him. The trading post was a distant dot.

Drawing the sorrel to a halt once more, he drew out his field glasses and swept the scene below. The trading post swam into his vision and he could clearly see the little mound that marked the Johnstons' grave. Then he picked out a rider. He watched him for a moment before putting the glasses back in their holder. There was nothing remarkable in that.

As he rode, he observed his surroundings closely, as he always did. It made sense to know the terrain. Occasionally he noticed more horse droppings, confirming that someone had ridden the trail before him. The country was good, with wide grass slopes and groves of aspen. Above him the slopes were lined with spruce and pine. The air was clear, and sounds seemed to travel a long distance; the tread of his horse's hoofs and the creak of his saddle sounded unusually loud. He came to a bend in the trail overhung by rocks, and a little way beyond found himself looking down upon a hollow that was just filling with the evening's shade. A stream ran along the bottom with clumps of aspen and willows along it. Shadows were lengthening and he decided that it would make a good place to set up camp for the night.

When he had chosen his spot, he ground-hitched the horse, allowing it freedom to graze, and began to collect brushwood for a fire. He lay slabs of bacon in his skillet and boiled up water from the stream for coffee. Once he had eaten, he settled back with a mug of coffee in his hand. There was a chill in the air and it felt good in the glow of the fire. The stars were bright and a yellow moon hung low. Occasionally the flames would flare up and throw into relief the horse grazing nearby. It was the sort of night to appreciate. As the fire began to flicker and fade, he lapsed into a slumber but he slept with one eye open and his hand was next to his rifle.

* * *

Tuplin's decision to ride up into the hills had not been an entirely random one. Prospectors or trappers might have passed that way, and he was hoping he might find the remains of a cabin where he could hole up for a while. Maybe he would even strike lucky and find gold. He followed the main trail high into the hills before branching out on a side trail which led up toward an escarpment. He didn't know much about these sorts of things, but it seemed to be the type of place that might contain gold-bearing quartz. It was a long shot that he would find the remains of a settlement, but he had nothing to lose. He would be no worse off than he would be anywhere else.

The silence of the hills was already beginning to get on his nerves. Although he had taken what he needed for the immediate future from the trading store, it wouldn't last indefinitely and he was feeling less confident by the moment that he would be able to live off the land. He certainly didn't intend staying long. Maybe leaving the Bar Seven had been one big mistake. There was no real reason to link him with the shooting of

Rimmer. Maybe . . . but it was no good regretting it now. Even if it had not been the case previously, the finger of suspicion was now firmly pointing at himself. There was no going back. And if anybody was on his trail, they wouldn't expect him to take to the hills. Why should anyone be on his trail? Was he being irrational? He tried to put away the thoughts that were ringing in his head, tried to concentrate on getting up to the escarpment.

The new trail led him through a pine forest. The thud of the horse's hoofs was muffled, and in places the trees grew so close together that there was scarcely room to pass. The pines gave way to spruce, and then the trees began to thin out. Above him, great shoulders of granite rose into the clear air. The trail he had been following through the timber was no longer clear, but he could detect a faint track leading along the side of the hill towards the solid rock wall of the escarpment. He brought the horse to a halt, straining his eyes to see ahead. He looked along the line of the escarpment. A dark penumbra of shadow made it difficult to pick things out, but he thought he saw what he was looking for. Partly hidden by clumps of vegetation, he could just make out a dilapidated hut. Encouraged, he spurred the horse onward once more, and presently was rewarded by the sight of a few more broken-down shacks and sheds, with what looked like the opening to a tunnel.

He rode up and dismounted. Darkness was falling and the place had an eerie atmosphere. He drew his six-gun and began to check through the buildings. They were all in an advanced stage of disrepair, but the one he had first seen, standing on its own a little apart from the others, seemed to be the most suitable. He checked once more and peered into the mouth of the tunnel. It seemed to hum like a shell when put to the ear. He was feeling nervous and a little scared. Maybe it would be better to camp out in the open. He stood irresolute for some time, looking anxiously around him, before eventually making the decision to stay.

*   *   *

Somewhere in the darkness Rimmer could hear the low voice of his fellow rider, a man called Peters, as he crooned to the cattle. He had pulled on his slicker and his Stetson was pulled over his eyes, but it didn't prevent him from getting wet. The two men were circling the herd in opposite directions, each straining against the driving rain. The cattle were still restless and some of them kept bawling. Rimmer didn't know why, but he felt edgy. In the darkness the black shape of a cow moved, and he edged it back into the herd. He rode slowly and presently the other rider loomed up out of the blackness.

'Sure is a bad night,' Peters said.

Rimmer nodded, although it was doubtful the other man would see the movement in the darkness.

'Take it slow and easy,' he said. 'Be careful not to do anythin' else that might spook 'em.'

'Sure thing,' Peters replied.

They continued riding, letting their horses go at their own pace, barely needing to touch the bridle reins. Rimmer was looking out for the first signs of dawn, when he suddenly jerked to attention, straining to listen. For a moment he could hear nothing except the hiss of the rain but then his ears picked up a faint sound. It took only a moment for him to realize it was made by galloping hoofs. At the same moment Peters came riding up again.

'You heard it too?' he said.

'Yup.'

They both listened but the sound had died away.

'Maybe we'd better roust up the men,' Peters said, 'or we could have a stampede on our hands.'

Rimmer glanced towards the herd.

'Don't do anything for a moment,' he replied.

They listened and the sound of hoof-beats came again. This time they weren't drumming and it was obvious that the riders were approaching with caution. Presently two shapes emerged from the darkness.

'Strike me!' Peters exclaimed, 'I think it's White and Fielding.'

Rimmer spurred his horse forward. Peters was right. The newcomers were two of the men he had left behind to run the Sawtooth.

'Sorry to arrive at this hour,' the first man said. 'Hope we didn't do anythin' to spook the cattle.'

'They'll be all right,' Rimmer replied. 'Just tell me what in tarnation you're doin' here.'

They gathered about the camp fire and the cook rustled up some beans and biscuits to go with a fresh brew of coffee. While they ate and drank White and Fielding explained what had happened back at the Sawtooth.

'We got here just as fast as we could,' Fielding said.

Rimmer had been silent, drinking coffee from his battered tin cup. Now he looked up at the others.

'Seems to me like Claridge ain't gonna be content with takin' over the Sawtooth. He caught us out there, but he must know we ain't gonna take it lyin' down. He knows we'll be back. I reckon the attack on the ranch is just part of it. Now he's gonna want to finish the job.'

'You figure he's plannin' to attack us?' someone asked.

'That's exactly what I think. We're at a disadvantage. He'll probably try to hit us at some weak point on the trail.'

He turned to one of the ranch-hands standing nearby.

'You've been up and down this trail more times than anyone,' he said. 'If you were Claridge, where would you choose?'

The man thought for a moment.

'We've got a river to cross not too far up ahead,' he replied. 'It's a branch of the Locust. That would be a good place. We'd be occupied in tryin' to swim those beeves across.'

He stopped and scratched his chin.

'There's another place that might suit even better,' he continued. 'It's a kind of gorge. The trail narrows to pass through. That would maybe be another spot.'

'Thanks for that,' Rimmer replied. He thought for a moment. 'OK,' he said, 'This is what we'll do.'

★ ★ ★

Stretton's eyes blinked open. He listened closely, but could hear nothing except the soughing of the wind in the trees. Reaching for his rifle, he got to his feet and moved away from the embers of the fire into the surrounding darkness. Something had awakened him, but he didn't know what. He remained immobile, his senses alert, as the minutes passed. There was no indication of anything untoward, but he felt uneasy. He had learned to trust his instincts, and they told him that he wasn't alone. Although he had no definite proof, he was convinced that someone or something was out there in the night.

Silently and stealthily he began to move around the perimeter of the camp, his eyes searching the blackness. Dim, dark shapes loomed and shadows flickered in the fading moonlight. After a considerable time had passed, he returned to his blanket, but he could not relax. Just beyond range of the firelight, outlined against the sky, his horse stamped and blew. Something was making it restless. It snorted once again and the subsequent silence seemed deeper than before. It was pointless to seek sleep again. After a while he rolled a cigarette and lay back with his head against the saddle and the rifle cradled in his arms till the first fingers of dawn began to reach into the hollow.

7

Rimmer kneeled behind a rock half-way up the side of the gorge and took out his field glasses to survey the country. Once he was satisfied the herd could not be seen, he put them back in their holder.

'Any sign of Claridge?' Lindop said.

'Nope. And even more to the point, there's no sign of the herd.'

'I hope we're right about Claridge taking the long route to get here,' Lindop said.

'It's a fair bet. A bunch of riders like he'll have with him kicks up a lot of dust. The last thing he would want would be to give us any warning he was on his way.'

'Seems to me we're takin' a few chances,' someone said.

'The cattle will be OK for now. We've left enough men to keep 'em in order. If some of 'em stray, we'll be able to round 'em up again once this little business is over with.'

'I don't know why you call it little,' another voice muttered. 'We're gonna be well outnumbered by Claridge's men. If they even get here, that is.'

'They'll get here. And once they do, we'll deal with them. We've got the drop on 'em. They won't be expectin' us to be here. We're taking up the very places they would have chosen. We'll take 'em by surprise.'

The choice of the gorge to make a stand was certainly right. It was a good spot. Rimmer looked out over the landscape. Far off he could just make out the course of the river they would have to cross. As trail boss, he had considered making that the place to meet Claridge, but it was too open; there was little in the way of vegetation that might be used for concealment, and they would have to deal with Claridge on level terms. No, this way he had control of the situation. Claridge

184

would be riding straight into a carefully prepared trap, the very trap he probably had in mind himself. The situation was reversed, and Rimmer was satisfied that he had done everything he could to gain the upper hand.

The rain that had presented so many problems previously had ceased, but the skies were still heavy and overhung. Rimmer and his men had taken up positions near the entrance to the gorge, and on the very summit one of the men was watching for any sign of Claridge and the Bar Seven boys. At last his voice rang out from on high:

'Get ready! They're on their way!'

The look-out scrambled down the hillside to join the others. Rimmer took another look through his field glasses but couldn't see anything. The look-out's words were confirmed, however, because presently they began to pick up the faint drumming of hoof-beats. Rimmer's features creased in a grim smile. He wasn't wrong. Claridge was heading for the gorge.

The sound of hoofs grew louder, though still muffled by the damp ground, and then the riders appeared, coming on at a steady trot. Rimmer got to his feet and began to move down the hillside.

'Are you sure about this?' Lindop asked.

Rimmer turned.

'We've already discussed it. I want to avoid bloodshed if I can.'

'You're takin' one hell of a risk. Claridge ain't likely to be in the mood to parley.'

'It's a risk I'm willin' to take. Maybe we can settle this whole thing. Claridge might still be open to reason.'

Rimmer scrambled down the slope till he was standing at the entrance to the gap. One of the men stepped out with his rifle and stood next to him. Rimmer glanced at him. He opened his mouth to say something but just nodded. Together, they awaited the arrival of Claridge and his men. The noise of horses' hoofs grew louder and louder, and then the riders appeared. They didn't seem to notice anything because they carried on riding till Claridge suddenly threw up his arm and they came to a disorderly halt. Taken by surprise, for a few moments they hesitated and then they began to come on again, moving slowly and reaching for their guns. When he was within a few yards of Rimmer, Claridge stopped.

'What is this?' he said. His tone of voice betrayed his uncertainty.

'I know what your game is,' Rimmer said.

'I don't know what you mean,' Claridge replied.

'I mean what I say. I've got men on the hillside. They've got their rifles pointed at you right now.'

Claridge raised himself in the stirrups and looked back at his men. They were looking worried and tense as they raised their eyes to the surrounding slopes.

'I suggest you save yourselves a whole heap of trouble and hand over your guns,' Rimmer said.

Claridge stroked his chin in a feeble

attempt at bravado, but Rimmer noticed his eyes flicker as he, too, glanced up at the slopes.

'I don't know what all this is about,' he said.

The words were scarcely out of his mouth when the tension was cut by a gunshot. The sound reverberated from the hillside. For a moment Rimmer looked away from Claridge to see a smoking gun in the hand of one of Claridge's men.

'Take cover!' he shouted.

At the same moment a rifle barked and a bullet flew past his shoulder. He and his companion dived for safety as the hillside erupted in fire and flame, and the whole scene disintegrated into a mêlée of panic and confusion. Horses reared and brayed. There was a scrimmage; some of Claridge's men turned and began to ride away, while others opened fire. Rimmer had taken cover behind the rocks and boulders which stood at the entrance to the gap. Glancing to his right, he saw the other man clutching his arm.

'Are you OK?' he shouted above the din.

The man nodded and shouted something back, but it was lost in the noise as bullets whined and ricocheted among the rocks. Rimmer scrambled his way further up the hillside and then began firing into the mêlée in front of him.

When his rifle was empty he threw it aside and began to blaze away with his six-guns. A furious cannonade resounded from the hillside above him. Bullets were clipping the rocks uncomfortably close by, and the whine of their ricochets sang in his ears. Shots were coming from all directions, and he was running the additional risk of being fired on from his own side. He felt a bullet tug at the sleeve of his jacket, but he carried on firing. Gunsmoke hung heavy in the air and it was difficult to make out what was happening with Claridge and his men. There was nothing to be done but to carry on shooting and keep his head down. He heard a clatter of hoofs and a riderless horse reared up in front of him, galloping down the gorge. A loud scream rang out above the gunfire and a body came crashing and rolling down the hillside. It wasn't just Claridge's men who were being killed or wounded.

He jammed more slugs into his guns, and as he did so he became aware that the noise of shooting had faded. It was more intermittent, but he wasn't sure what it portended. Very slowly, he raised his head above the level of the rock and looked towards the opening to the gap. Bodies of men and horses lay sprawled across the grass. Gunfire still sounded intermittently from somewhere beyond but it didn't amount to much. Lowering his head again, he looked up the hillside. Odd spurts of flame indicated the presence of his men.

'It's Rimmer!' he shouted. 'Can you see anything?'

The voice of Lindop rang out in reply.

'There ain't any left alive. If there are, it looks like they've skedaddled.' As if to deny his statement, there was a rattle of gunfire aimed at the hillside, followed by some answering shots. The ensuing silence was short-lived. Soon there came the sound of hoof-beats, which vanished into the distance.

'It's a couple of Claridge's men,' Lindop called. 'They're out of range.'

'Let 'em go,' Rimmer shouted back.

Slowly he got to his feet, and emerging from cover, started to make his way to where the bodies lay. Some of the Sawtooth men did likewise, scrabbling their way down the hill. A scene of carnage met their eyes. Horses and men lay entangled together. Rimmer quickly did a body count before turning to the others coming up behind him.

'How about our boys?' he asked.

'There's one dead for sure. A couple of them received hits but they'll be OK,' Lindop said. 'There's one unaccounted for — Burrage.'

'I saw someone fall from up there,' Rimmer said. 'That must be him.'

He turned back to make his way to

where he calculated Burrage must have landed. When he reached him he found he was wounded but still alive. One leg was twisted beneath him but he was conscious.

'Did we win?' Burrage asked.

'Yup.'

The youngster let out a loud groan.

'Try not to move,' Rimmer said.

He gently opened Burrage's shirt. He had taken a bullet in the upper arm but it didn't look serious. His leg was more of a concern, but Rimmer wasn't lying when he reassured the youth that he would pull through.

Later, they all assembled at the mouth of the gap. Although they had won the day, the mood was subdued. Burrage's wound had been treated as well as they knew how, and a rough travois had been put together to carry him back. Their horses had been gathered and they were saddled and ready to go. Lindop shook each man's hand.

'I thank you for what you've done today,' he said.

'They signed to the brand,' Rimmer replied.

'We ain't finished yet,' another man said.

'Creighton's right,' Lindop said. 'Now we've got to get back to the Sawtooth and clean out the rest of the varmints.'

* * *

Morning broke, and after a quick breakfast, Stretton carried on riding. He was looking out for clues, but when he couldn't find any, he began to wonder whether he had gone wrong somewhere. Perhaps there was a side trail he had ignored. He brought his horse to a halt and sat pondering what he should do. He took out his field glasses and swept the terrain. Away to his right was a steep escarpment, and beneath it he thought he could make out some darker shapes, which might be huts. There didn't seem to be much else. Maybe it was worth retracing his steps and seeing if there was a way up. Replacing the glasses, he turned the sorrel and began to head back the way he had come.

As he rode, he began to have an uncomfortable feeling that someone was watching him. It was the same sensation he had had the previous night, that he was not alone. He stopped again and took another look through his field glasses but could see no sign of anything moving, no indication of someone else being there besides himself. He put the glasses back, deciding that the impression must be down to nerves. Yet he felt perfectly calm. After a time he found what he was looking for, a trail that led towards the escarpment, and took it.

As he rode, a thin rain began to fall. The trail became slippery and he took care with the horse. He leaned slightly forward in the saddle, looking for any signs of someone having passed that way. It wasn't long till he found horse droppings. Now he was more certain that he was on the right track. Gradually, the escarpment came nearer, and when he stopped once more to take a look through his field glasses, he could clearly see the remains of the mining camp. He looked about him. The wind sighed and the landscape seemed to whisper with the pattering of the rain. Visibility was not good, but he kept looking about him, still having the feeling that eyes were on him. When he was still some little way from the deserted mining camp, he drew his horse to a halt and stepped out of the leather. If there was a chance that Tuplin might have taken refuge in one of the huts, he needed to be cautious, and that meant going the rest of the way on foot. He knee-haltered the animal where it would be well out of sight before continuing his climb.

When he was in sight of the huts, he crouched in some bushes to take stock. If Tuplin was around, where was he likely to be? He examined the scene closely. Some huts stood together, but another one stood slightly apart. Built against it were the remains of a lean-to which had at one time possibly served as a stable. It was largely a matter of chance, but it seemed slightly more promising than the others. Taking his six-gun in his hand, he crept slowly and carefully towards it, keeping to whatever vegetation offered some chance of concealment. He hadn't gone far when he heard the muted stamp of a horse's hoof. He glanced behind him, thinking that some rider was creeping up on him. Then he realized that the sound had come from within the lean-to stable. Taking a closer look, he could in fact discern the vague outline of a horse.

Taking even greater care, he crept up to the cabin and flattened himself against the wall, listening intently. The rain continued to fall, spattering on the sagging roof of the building. He heard a shuffling of hoofs from within the lean-to, and crept forward. But the ground was getting soggy, and as he did so his boot slipped and he staggered sideward. At almost the same instant there suddenly came a stab of flame and the report of a rifle, and a bullet went flying past his shoulder. If he hadn't slipped, he would have taken the bullet full on.

In a moment his six-gun was in his hand and he returned fire. A second bullet crashed into the wall beside him. Because of the dim light and the rain it was hard to see anything clearly. He had a brief view of a vague figure before it disappeared around a corner of the building. Inside the lean-to stable the horse began to whinny. He ran forward in pursuit, and as he came round the building he was met by a hail of gunfire. He dropped to one knee and quickly loosed a couple of shots, but the man had gone again. In that brief moment he had a better view. The man was small and he was sure it could only be Tuplin.

Scrambling to his feet, he began to charge after him once more but then suddenly stopped. He seemed to be chasing Tuplin round the cabin. If he went in the other direction, maybe he would catch him by surprise. Quickly, he doubled back till he was at a corner of the building, where he stopped and crouched down, waiting for Tuplin. He seemed to be waiting that way for a long time and he was beginning to think he had been wrong when Tuplin suddenly appeared, almost on top of him. Instinctively he stuck out a leg and Tuplin went tumbling over, dropping his six-gun in the process. Rimmer leaped to his feet, and as Tuplin struggled to reach his gun, stepped hard on his arm. Tuplin let out a howl of pain and then looked up to see Stretton's six-gun pointed at his chest.

'Don't shoot! Please don't shoot!' Tuplin began to babble.

Stretton bent down and lowered the gun so it was close to Tuplin's face.

'Please!' Tuplin begged.

His face was contorted with fear and tears began to flow down his cheek. Suddenly Stretton wasn't interested any more. He had an almost physical sensation of something flowing from him, and he felt empty and drained. He gazed at the gun in his hand as if it were something alien, as though he didn't know what it was doing there. Almost unconsciously he placed it in his holster, and barely had enough presence of mind to pick up Tuplin's gun. Tuplin was squirming on the ground and Stretton dragged him to his feet.

'Tell me one thing,' he said. 'Was it you who shot Crowther?'

'I didn't mean to. I couldn't help it. I had no choice.'

Suddenly his tone changed.

'I can help you,' he mumbled. 'I can tell you about Claridge.'

'What about Claridge?'

'Promise me . . . '

Before he could go any further Stretton seized him by the throat.

'I said: what about Claridge?'

'He's plannin' to attack the Sawtooth. He's only been waitin' for Lindop to start on the cattle drive.'

Stretton pushed him aside. The man was a liar, but he knew that this time he was telling the truth. He had an almost overwhelming sense of failure. He had made all the wrong choices. He might have gone under but for one thing. He knew where his only chance of salvation lay. Now only one thing mattered to him. He needed to get back to the Sawtooth as quickly as possible. He looked once at Tuplin and began to move away, but he had barely taken a few steps when the silence was shattered by the roar of a gun. He turned in an instant to see Tuplin staggering backwards. There was a second blast, and then he saw that they had been joined by someone else: the man stood with a gun in his hand. It was the man with the braid who had been present at the trading post.

'You killed Johnston!' the man yelled. 'Now it's your turn.'

Tuplin was still standing, his hands clutched to his stomach. When he moved them a fountain of blood sprang out, and he slowly crumpled to the floor. As Stretton continued to watch in horror the newcomer moved rapidly towards Tuplin and emptied another bullet into his prostrate form. Stretton remained immobile for another instant before being restored to movement. He moved to where the man with the braid still stood over Tuplin's dead body.

'You followed me up here,' he said. 'I had a feelin' I was bein' watched. It was you I sensed.'

The man looked up at him.

'Yes,' he said. 'I followed you. I wasn't goin' to let this skunk get away with it. I wanted to make sure he paid for what he did.'

Stretton looked at him, not knowing what to say. He glanced down once at Tuplin's bleeding corpse and then, without another word, he walked away.

* * *

Stretton's one desire was to get back to the Sawtooth as quickly as possible, but the trail back down the hillside was treacherous and he had no intention of putting his horse at risk. It took a concentrated effort to restrain his impatience, but he made his way slowly, holding the animal back at times. It seemed to take a long time, but eventually he reached more level ground and was able to go faster. He crossed the ford without mishap, and when he got to the other side, he decided to by-pass the trading post. It was partly out of a reluctance to see it again, but more because he figured that if he took a slightly different route, he might get to the Sawtooth quicker. He was taking a risk. He didn't know the country or what obstacles there might be, but he trusted his sense of direction and determined to take the chance.

Once he had reached the decision, he applied his spurs to the horse's flanks and it stretched out into a gallop. It seemed to relish the opportunity to run freely, and he gave it its head. He carried on that way till he felt the horse begin to tire, when he slowed it down and continued at a steadier pace. He knew that to let the sorrel get blown would be counter-productive. There was a long way to go, and it seemed to get longer by the hour. After a time he stopped and dismounted to let the horse rest further and then he climbed back into leather and urged it to another gallop. The horse strained forward, and when he slowed it again it showed its reluctance by tugging at the bit.

The part of the country he was riding through was growing rougher, with sage grass and patches of mesquite. He began to have doubts about whether he had done the right thing after all, opting for an alternative way back to the Sawtooth. What was going on there now? He didn't like to think too much about what might have happened, and he cursed himself for having left when he did. He had deserted his friends when they needed him most. His sense of guilt expanded, and he began to blame himself for what had happened to Rimmer and Lana. It was because of him they had both been injured. He had brought with him nothing but trouble. The only crumb of comfort left to him was to try and undo what he had done, to make amends for all his wrong actions and mistakes. Was it already too late? He could only hope and pray that time and opportunity were still left to him.

He was on the right track after all. As he rode, he began to notice landmarks that looked vaguely familiar, and he realized that at last he was closing in on the Sawtooth. He had taken care to nurse his horse along, and even though he was nearing exhaustion himself, the fact seemed to give him fresh strength. He continued his inexorable progress till he thought he heard something, and brought the sorrel to a halt in order to listen more closely. A few minutes passed, and then a change in wind direction brought a noise to his ears: the sound of gunfire. It was faint, but there was no mistaking it. Muttering a curse under his breath, he spurred his horse and it burst forward.

He didn't know exactly what was going on, but the gunshots spelt trouble. It could only be that the Sawtooth was under attack. He was right: Tuplin hadn't been lying. In a short space of time he had his first view of the ranch-house, but he could also see plumes of smoke issuing from various spots where the gunmen had taken cover. He was thinking rapidly. Should he stop and dismount, or did he dare burst through the surrounding fire and try to make it to the ranch-house? Making a quick decision, he brought his horse to a shuddering halt and jumped from the saddle. Grabbing his rifle, he took shelter behind some bushes.

No sooner had he done so than a crescendo of gunfire came from the direction of the ranch. Bullets tore up the ground in front of him, and he looked about for a better position. The outburst was followed by a moment of silence, and through it he heard the sound of hoofs. Some horsemen were coming up behind him. He crouched low, hoping they would not see him, but prepared to try and fight them off if he needed to. They were kicking up a good deal of dust, but as they got nearer he could begin to make out some of their features, and he gave a gasp of surprise: far from being Bar Seven men, it was Rimmer in the forefront. He had assumed that the Sawtooth was under attack from Claridge, so didn't know quite what to make of this new situation, but he needed to let Rimmer know he was there.

Fortunately, Rimmer seemed to come to the same conclusion as Stretton had himself: rather than carry on into the heart of the skirmish, the riders halted and began to dismount. Taking advantage of the situation, Stretton stood up and began to wave his arms frantically and call his name. The first response took the form of a bullet, which went whining overhead, but then he heard someone shout something and there was no second shot. Still calling, he stepped forward and began to make his way towards them.

'Hell, it's Stretton!' Rimmer shouted.

In a moment they were shaking one another by the hand.

'I'm sorry,' Stretton said. At that moment there was fresh outburst of gunfire from the direction of the ranch-house.

'Leave it till later,' Rimmer said. 'That's Claridge's men in there. Lindop and a few of our boys got into position here and obviously decided to have a go. We were lookin' to come in by the back door but they've got it covered.'

'I'm not sure I get it.'

'The explanations can come later. Right now we need to figure out how to prise Claridge from the ranch-house.'

Turning to the others, he ordered them to take cover. As gunshots boomed and a fresh wave of bullets flew through the air, they didn't delay any further in doing so.

Stretton took up the position he had occupied before Rimmer's arrival; from there he had a good overall view of the situation. Most of the shooting from Claridge's men was coming from the ranch-house itself, but there was also some from the outbuildings. Claridge had obviously stationed some of his men in them. That was probably the reason Rimmer had been deterred from riding down on the ranch-house. He observed them closely. It seemed to him that if he could take over one of the larger barns, he might be in an excellent position to pour down his fire from close range and at an angle Claridge might find hard to defend. He cast his eye over the terrain. It offered a reasonable amount of cover.

He began to edge forward, keeping low. As he advanced, he came in sight of a couple of the Sawtooth men, and he acknowledged their presence with a gesture. The gunfire had become intermittent, but suddenly there was another outburst and he took advantage of the situation to make a sprint for the barn.

He stood for a few moments, pressed against the side of the building. When he looked up, he saw the muzzle of a rifle protruding through an aperture. One of Claridge's gunmen must have taken up position on an upper floor. Quickly he slid to the front of the barn and flung himself through the doorway. It was comparatively dark inside, and it took a few moments for his eyes to adjust. Then he saw that the barn had an upper storey. Light filtered through a hatchway and fell on a ladder, which had toppled to one side. He considered retrieving it for a moment, but quickly realized how impractical the idea was. He could make a pretty good guess as to where the gunman was placed, and he determined to take a chance.

Creeping silently to the back of the barn, he positioned himself, raised his rifle, and squeezed the trigger. The effect was instantaneous as the bullet crashed through the floorboards, and was answered by a startled exclamation and the thud of boots. Stretton fired again, and then part of the man's frame appeared in the aperture. There was a flash and a deafening roar as the man's gun spoke. A bullet hit the floor inches from where Stretton was standing, but he remained steady as he squeezed the trigger once more. The bullet flew wide, thudding into the roof of the barn, but as the man above stepped aside he lost his footing and came crashing to the floor of the barn. He lay face down for a moment in a crumpled heap before letting out a muffled gasp and beginning to get to his knees. He was obviously badly winded, and he remained doubled over for a few moments. When he finally looked up, it was Stretton's turn to gasp.

'Yoakum!' he exclaimed.

The injured man's gun had fallen to one side and he reached out to retrieve it but Stretton kicked it aside. Yoakum was breathing heavily, trying to draw air into his lungs. With an effort he finally struggled to his feet.

'All right, Stretton,' he said. 'Looks like you win.'

Stretton regarded him steadily.

'Nobody wins,' he said.

'Why don't you go ahead and shoot me? It's what you've been wantin' to do.'

In spite of himself, Stretton couldn't help admiring the man's attitude.

'I know now you didn't kill Crowther,' Stretton replied. 'I was wrong. I admit it. I apologise.'

It struck him that it was the second time he had done so in a short space of time, but it didn't make him feel any better. Yoakum looked at him with a puzzled expression on his face.

'Why did you ever think I did?'

'Never mind.'

They continued to look at one another, while outside the rattle of gunfire resumed.

'I've nothin' against you,' Stretton said. 'Hell, there's no reason we should be fightin' each other.' He walked across to where the rifle lay on the floor and picked it up.

'I'd be tempted to give you this back,' he said. 'But I ain't quite that trustin'. Right now I'm walkin' back through that door. The way I figure it, the best thing for you would be to do the same and just keep on goin'.'

He moved to the entrance and peered outside. The sounds of gunfire had dwindled again. He was about to make his exit when Yoakum spoke.

'You know that Claridge has already made a run for it?'

Stretton turned his head.

'It's true. He's headed for town.'

'Then why are you still here?'

'I didn't seem to have much choice while the fightin' was in full swing, but I figure it's over. I'd say the time's about come to take up your advice.'

Stretton wasn't sure whether to believe Yoakum or not, but there didn't seem to be any point in lying.

'I reckon I know where you can find him,' Yoakum said.

'Oh yeah? Go on.'

'Unless I'm completely mistaken, he'll be at the Eagle Saloon.'

Stretton didn't respond. Instead, he took one last long look at Yoakum, and then ducked quickly outside and made his way along the side of the barn. He was working out what his next move should be when a horseman suddenly appeared from the runway at the back of the stables. His horse reared, but he quickly brought it under control and began to ride away. Stretton was taken aback and barely noticed as a little group of men burst from the ranch-house, running pell-mell in different directions. They drew a burst of gunfire and two of them fell. The noise of the gunshots brought him back to earth. It looked like Yoakum was right. Claridge's men appeared to have called it a day. He ran forward to get closer to the stables. A shot went whistling by, but he had no idea where it came from. Crouching low, he approached the building and peered inside. The place was deserted. The few horses that remained in the stalls carried the Bar Seven brand. As he carefully made his way to the back, he heard footsteps behind him and spun round.

'Rimmer!' he exclaimed.

The foreman stood dangerously outlined against the daylight. His gun was in his hand.

In a few moments he was joined by a few others coming up behind him.

'Stretton,' he replied. 'You're lucky I didn't shoot.'

Stretton straightened up.

'You were taking a chance yourself,' he replied.

Rimmer and his men entered the barn and advanced to meet Stretton.

'Well,' Rimmer said, 'I think the fighting's over. The Sawtooth is back in our hands.'

The men let out a cheer.

'Where's Lindop?' Stretton asked.

'He's gone to make sure Burrage is OK.'

In response to the blank look on Stretton's face, Rimmer quickly explained what had happened at the gap.

'Apart from takin' a bullet, Burrage had a nasty fall,' he said. 'I know you and he made a good team. Once he's recovered, I figure you can carry on that way.'

For a moment Stretton and Rimmer both hesitated, and then they embraced.

'Good to have you back on board,' Rimmer said.

It took a while for things to settle down. The ranch-house had taken a battering, and not only as a result of the gunfight. Claridge's men had caused a fair amount of damage themselves. When order had been restored, Lindop and Rimmer took advantage of the time to relax, while the men celebrated in the bunkhouse.

'Make the most of it,' Rimmer said. 'We've got to be back on the trail tomorrow.'

'I hope the boys we left behind are not havin' any trouble with the beeves,' Lindop replied.

'I wouldn't worry about that. They're a good crew. They know what they're doin'.'

'They must be wonderin' what's become of us.'

Rimmer took a long sip from the glass of whiskey he held in his hand.

'You don't figure Claridge will give us any more trouble?' he asked.

'Nope. I think he'll have learned his

lesson. I don't know what will become of the Bar Seven, because he's gonna be facin' a good spell in jail.'

'I wouldn't count on Malone doin' his duty. He and Claridge are hand-in-glove.'

'That might have been the case, but now that Claridge is on the losin' side, I have a feelin' Malone's attitude is about to change. I'm not sure there was ever too much love between them. If he doesn't enforce the law, I figure the good citizens of Buckstrap are goin' to have somethin' to say about it.'

Lindop glanced towards the door leading into the room in which Burrage lay in bed propped against the pillows.

'Stretton is spendin' some time in there,' he said. 'He doesn't want to tire Burrage out.'

As if he had heard Lindop's comment, Stretton suddenly appeared in the doorframe.

'He's asleep,' he said.

'That's good. We'll get the doc to look him over tomorrow.'

'Have a drink,' Rimmer said.

'Here, let me get it,' Lindop added. He got to his feet, poured a drink and handed it to Stretton.

'You don't seem too happy, considerin' we won the day,' Rimmer commented.

'I'm fine. Just kinda tired, that's all.'

'It's been quite a time,' Lindop said.

He and Rimmer exchanged glances. Silence fell in the room, broken by the sounds of celebration outside. When their glasses were empty, Lindop got up and refreshed them and they carried on drinking, each seemingly lost in his own thoughts. Presently Rimmer looked up at Stretton.

'Why don't you take a ride into town? If not now, maybe tomorrow?'

'Why should I do that?' Stretton replied.

'I know you've been concerned about Lana. Since she got shot, I mean.'

'I gather she's made a good recovery. Besides, there isn't time. You said yourself we've got to get on with drivin' that herd to the railhead.'

'Somebody has to go, just to make sure Claridge gets his desserts.'

Lindop got to his feet and moved to the door. He opened it and looked outside. The noise from the bunk-house grew louder.

'Sure is a fine night,' he said. 'It's a relief after all that rain.'

He peered out into the darkness. The land was bathed in moonshine. He was about to turn back inside when he saw something in the distance: it was a rider, and as it got closer he could distinguish who it was. He turned back and called over his shoulder to Stretton:

'No need to go into town. There's someone heading this way now, and it's Lana.'